W. E. Baldwin

Essential Lessons in Human Physiology and Hygiene for Schools

W. E. Baldwin

Essential Lessons in Human Physiology and Hygiene for Schools

ISBN/EAN: 9783337361716

Printed in Europe, USA, Canada, Australia, Japan

Cover: Foto ©Andreas Hilbeck / pixelio.de

More available books at **www.hansebooks.com**

THE WERNER EDUCATIONAL SERIES

ESSENTIAL LESSONS

IN

HUMAN PHYSIOLOGY

AND HYGIENE

FOR SCHOOLS

By WINFRED E. BALDWIN, M. D.
Author of "Primary Lessons in Human Physiology," etc.

AMERICAN BOOK COMPANY
NEW YORK   CINCINNATI   CHICAGO

PREFACE.

In the preparation of the following chapters on human physiology and hygiene, the author has attempted to present only such facts as are essential to the most practical knowledge of the subject—that is, such facts as people in the common walks of life most need to know, and such facts as all can remember and make use of whenever occasion demands. The plan of the work is such as adapts it to the needs, not only of intermediate classes in graded schools, but of the large number of pupils in the country schools where the time which can be devoted to the study of this subject is necessarily limited. As a general rule, an effort has been made to speak briefly and to the point, without unnecessary verbiage ; and, wherever such could be done without sacrificing accuracy or clearness of statement, rigid condensation has been practiced. It is believed, however, that this will not detract from the interest of the narrative or from the practical worth of the lessons. Many interesting facts, especially in anatomy, have been ruled out as not being knowledge of value to those for whom the book is intended. As the purpose and end of all such studies is the inculcation of rules and principles for the preservation of health, anatomy and physiology are throughout made subservient to hygiene and hygienic precepts.

Technical terms have been avoided as far as possible. Instead of confronting the learner with a pre-

liminary chapter of definitions—such as is often found
in text-books of this kind—and thus obliging him at the
outset to master a number of disconnected and, to him,
meaningless statements, the more common terms and
expressions peculiar to anatomy or physiology are explained in alphabetical order at the end of the book.
By this plan, the greater number of formal definitions
are omitted from the regular lessons, and all are placed
where they are most convenient for ready reference
whenever required.

Especial attention is given to the effects of alcohol,
tobacco, and other stimulants and narcotics upon the
human system, thus adapting the work to the requirements of the law in several of the states. The supplementary chapters on emergencies and the care of the
sick-room contain brief and simple directions, such as
every boy or girl should learn when young and remember all through life. The growing demand for school
instruction regarding the prevention of contagious and
communicable diseases—a demand which has found
formal expression in the laws of at least one of the
states of the Union—has induced the author to add a
third supplementary chapter on that subject. Here, as
in the other portions of the book, he has endeavored
to state his message briefly, and to give that kind of
information which every person can utilize and apply to
the benefit of himself and those around him. It is
knowledge of this kind, succinctly given, that imparts
to the following chapters their distinctive character as
essential lessons in human physiology and hygiene.

NEW YORK, 1896.

CONTENTS.

6 CONTENTS.

INTRODUCTION.

PHYSIOLOGY is the science which treats of and describes the action and functions of the various parts and organs of the body. In its most general meaning it has to do with all forms of life, both animal and vegetable. That division of the science which relates to the human body alone is called human physiology.

Anatomy is the science which treats of and describes the situation and the appearance of the component parts of the body. A general knowledge of the more common facts of anatomy is essential to a clear understanding of physiology, just as a knowledge of the structure and appearance of any object helps us to acquire a clearer comprehension of the nature and uses of that object.

Hygiene is the study which relates to the laws of health. It tells us how to take care of our bodies in such a way as to promote the health and strength of the organs composing them, and warns us against practices and habits which would be injurious to our physical well-being, or would prevent the full and harmonious development of all the parts and organs.

These three studies, physiology, anatomy, and hygiene, are very closely related, each really depending upon or supplementing the others. They teach the most important facts that can be learned about our physical nature: how our bodies are made, and how to preserve them from injury or disease. Many lives are lost or destroyed every day through ignorance of these facts.

A correct knowledge of the laws of health and of the structure of the human body warns us against breathing foul air and eating injurious foods; against using a sprained limb before it is able to perform its usual duties; against abusing the eyes through carelessness or by overwork; against neglecting what appears to be slight affections of various organs; and above all against the use of those insidious and powerful enemies to good health and human happiness, alcohol and tobacco, the effects of which are such that they invariably tend to weaken the body and render it subject to disease. Such knowledge also enables one to determine what to do, and do quickly, in cases of accidents or other emergencies; it gives plain, sensible directions for the care of the sick; and it shows how diseases, especially contagious or communicable diseases, may be avoided.

A general diffusion of such knowledge among the people, and especially among those who are still in the vigor of youth and untrammeled by health-destroying habits, will doubtless produce untold benefits. If a judicious and practical application is made of the precepts derived from such knowledge, it will certainly result not only in saving many lives from disease and death, but in promoting the health, strength, and happiness of all who are brought within the radius of its influence. The importance, therefore, of the study of the essential facts of physiology, anatomy, and hygiene cannot well be overestimated.

HUMAN PHYSIOLOGY.

✖

CHAPTER I.

BONE—ITS COMPOSITION AND USES.

1. Properties of Bone.—Bone, as we usually see it, is dead bone and is of a uniformly white color. In the living body, however, it is quite different, being of a pinkish-white color on the outside and deep red within. It is one of the hardest substances in the human body. Besides being hard, it is somewhat elastic, and is capable of standing a very great strain without being broken. It is exceedingly strong, and can bear greater pressure than the toughest oak wood.

2. Structure of Bone.—If a section of bone be examined, it will be seen that it is made up of two parts, or tissues.* One part is dense and compact, and looks very much like ivory. This is called the compact tissue. The other part is light and spongy, consisting of numerous fibers curiously interwoven together. This is called the cancellous or spongy tissue. The outer surface of all the bones is of compact tissue, which forms a dense shell of varying thickness around the cancellous tissue within. Where it is necessary

* See Definitions, p. 190.

that the bone should be very strong, it is largely made up of compact tissue. This is the case with the bones of the arms and the legs. Where lightness as well as strength is desirable, the bone is composed mostly of spongy or cancellous tissue, as in the small bones of

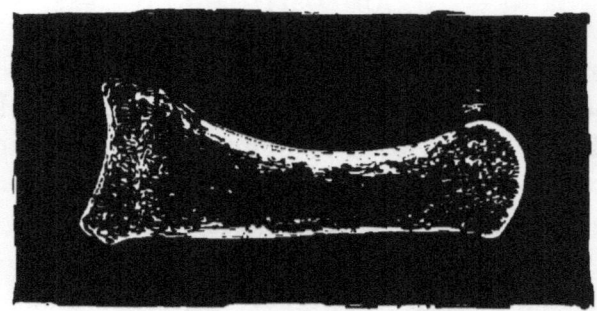

Fig. 1.—A section of bone showing the compact tissue at the borders and the spongy tissue within.

the hands and the feet, and in the enlarged ends of some other bones.

3. Composition of Bone.—It has already been said that bone is both hard and elastic; these properties are given to it by two widely different substances, of which it is chiefly composed.

One of these substances is earthy or inorganic, the other is animal or organic. The earthy or inorganic part of bone comprises about two-thirds of its weight, and is the part which gives to it its hardness. The animal or organic part of bone comprises about one third of its weight, and is the part which gives to it its elasticity and toughness.

Experiment.—Put a bone into a hot fire and let it stay there a few minutes, and then carefully remove it. It is still of the same shape as before, but it is much lighter. The reason of this is that the animal or organic part has been burned out of it, leaving only the earthy or inorganic part. It is now white and very brittle, and is easily broken or crushed. It is but little different from common lime.

Now take another bone—a long, slender bone is the best—and immerse it for some time in any dilute mineral acid, as dilute muriatic acid. The acid eats out the earthy part, but does not affect the animal part. The bone has still its original shape, but it is lighter in weight, and is soft and so pliable that it may easily be twisted or even tied in a knot.

4. Bone in the Young and in the Aged.—The composition of bone, as regards the relative amount of earthy and animal matter, varies at different periods of life.

In the bones of very young persons there is a greater proportion of animal matter, and this causes them to be soft and very elastic. Consequently, these bones will bend, but they are very difficult to break. In the aged the bones are very largely made up of lime, or earthy matter, and are, therefore, hard and brittle. These bones do not bend, but they are easily broken.

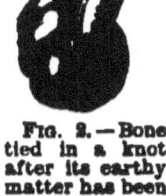

Fig. 2.—Bone tied in a knot after its earthy matter has been removed.

Thus it often happens that a child may have a heavy fall, without any serious injury; but if an old person should have the same fall, he would suffer with one or more broken bones.

5. Growth and Development of Bone.—In infancy the skeleton or framework of the body consists almost al-

together of *cartilage*, the white, glistening substance often called gristle.   As the body becomes older, earthy
matter is deposited in the cartilage, and bone is gradually developed, becoming harder, and growing propor-
tionately to the other parts of the body.   It is supplied
with nourishment in the same manner as the other parts'
of the body.   One's bones do not reach their full development until one is about twenty-five years old.

6. Uses of Bone.—If it were not for the bones, the
body would be merely a soft, shapeless mass ; hence
one very important use of the bones is to give to the
body firmness and a definite form.   Some of the
bones afford protection to the delicate organs * which
they partially enclose.   Some act as levers and, with
the muscles which are attached to them, give to the
body its power of movement.

7. The Periosteum.—Surrounding each bone, and closely covering it, is a tough fibrous membrane,* called
the *periosteum*.   In this periosteum there are a number
of small blood-vessels which penetrate into the substance
of the bone, and carry nourishment to it.   The periosteum
is of the greatest importance to the preservation and
development of the bones.   If it is bruised, or removed
from any part of a bone, or if it becomes diseased,
the bone ceases to be properly nourished, and soon
dies.

The periosteum is necessary to the formation of
new bone.   It is a well-known fact that a portion
of bone may be removed from the body, and if the
periosteum is not also removed, or seriously injured,
new bone will soon be formed to replace that which has

* See Definitions.

been taken away. If, however, the periosteum be removed, no new bone will be formed.

Some of the bones—especially the long, round ones—are hollow. The hollow space is filled with a fatty substance called *marrow*.

8. Diseases and Injuries of the Bones.—The bones are liable to many diseases which hinder their proper growth and development. Rickets is a disease in which the bones lack a proper amount of earthy matter, and are so soft as to be readily bent out of shape, thus causing many deformities of the body.

Children should not be allowed to stand upon their feet at too early an age, for the bones are then soft, and bend easily, and the deformity known as bow-legs is almost sure to result.

Bones are frequently injured, sometimes by being severely bruised, and sometimes by being broken. A bruised bone is often a most serious affair, especially so if the periosteum be severely injured. In such a case partial or complete death of the bone sometimes follows.

Accidents very often happen by which bones are broken. If a broken bone is properly set, that is, if the broken ends are rightly and skilfully placed together and kept there, it soon grows whole again, and becomes as strong and as useful as it was before the injury. Carelessness or ignorance in the setting of broken bones is quite sure to produce deformity. Only a skilful physician, or surgeon, therefore, should be entrusted with this duty.

9. Effects of Alcohol and Tobacco on the Bones.—When we speak of alcohol we mean alcoholic drinks—that is, all drinks which contain alcohol in any quantity, whether small or great. Hard cider, beer, ale, wine, whisky, brandy, and rum, are drinks of this class.

Any kind of alcoholic drink, when taken internally, is likely to produce harmful consequences to the person who indulges in its use. The bones receive their nourishment from the blood, and if this blood is changed in any way, so as to have less nourishing power, then the growth and development of the bones is hindered, or sometimes stopped altogether. Now, alcohol does this very thing; that is, it weakens the nourishing power of the blood, and its injurious effects on the bones are well known. These effects are especially marked in young and growing persons, where every part of the body needs the best nourishment possible.

It requires a much longer time for broken bones to heal in a person who is given to the use of alcoholic drinks than in one who is not. The same is true of other injuries to the bones; for here, too, the best of nourishment and plenty of pure blood are needed to promote recovery, and neither is supplied in persons who indulge in alcoholic drinks.

Tobacco also has a deleterious effect upon the nourishment and development of the bones. Its habitual use by young and growing persons is especially injurious. While interfering with the general nutrition of the body, it interferes also with the nutrition of the bones; and proper nourishment not being given, the growth of the bones is stunted, and their proper development is hindered. Boys who use tobacco in any form cannot expect to become as vigorous men as they might if they had never touched it.

CHAPTER II.

THE SKELETON.

10. The Skeleton.—The bones of the human body are so arranged and joined together as to form a framework upon which the other parts of the body are built and supported. This framework of bones is called the *skeleton*. There are about two hundred bones in the human skeleton, and these are joined to one another by means of *ligaments* and *cartilages*. The ligaments and cartilages, although they are not bone, are necessary to the construction of the skeleton, for they serve to hold the various bones together, and keep them in their proper places. The ligaments are strong bands of fibrous tissue; the cartilages are soft, glistening substances, forming what is commonly called gristle. The framework of the living human body, therefore, is formed of three different structures—bones, ligaments, and cartilages.

11. Classification of Bones.—The bones of the skeleton are divided into four classes :—

(1) Long bones;
(2) Short bones;
(3) Flat bones;
(4) Irregular bones.

The long bones, besides having other uses, act as levers, aiding in the movement of the different parts of the body. They are found in the legs and the arms, the fingers and toes.

The short bones are composed mostly of cancellous or spongy tissue, and are found in the hands and the feet, where lightness is necessary.

The flat bones are chiefly used for the protection of softer parts of the body. Such are the principal bones of the skull, which serve to encase and protect the brain.

The irregular bones have not only various shapes but various uses. The bones of the face and those of the backbone are examples.

12. Groups of Bones.—For convenience of study, the bones of the skeleton are divided into three groups:—

(1) The bones of the head;
(2) The bones of the trunk;
(3) The bones of the extremities.

13. The Bones of the Head.—The bones of the head form what is known as the skull. The skull comprises the face, and a hollow, bony case for holding the brain. This latter portion of the skull is called the *cranium*, and consists of eight bones. Its walls are composed of flat bones, which are very strong.

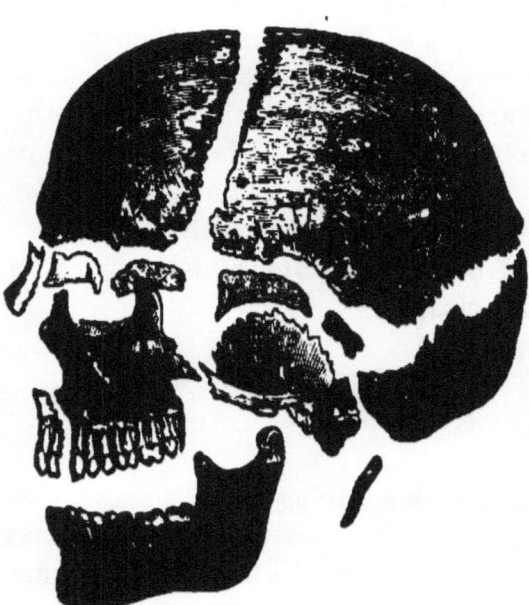

FIG. 3.—BONES OF THE HEAD.

These bones are joined together by tooth-like edges, those of each bone locking into those of another just as pieces of carpenter-work are dovetailed together. The point where two or more bones are thus fastened together is called a *suture*.

The bones of the face are fourteen in number; they are irregular in shape and are united by sutures. The only movable bone in the face is the lower jaw. The bones of the face are so arranged as to give position and shape to the mouth, the nose, the prominence of the cheeks, and the eye sockets.

14. Bones of the Trunk.—The trunk comprises all the body except the head and the upper and lower extremities.

The backbone, or spinal column, is the chief support of the trunk. It is composed of twenty-four small irregular bones, piled one upon another, forming a strong pillar upon which is supported the head. These small bones are called *vertebræ*. The vertebræ are of such a shape that when they are all placed one upon another, a canal, or circular passage, is formed extending through almost the whole length of the backbone, or spinal column. Through this canal

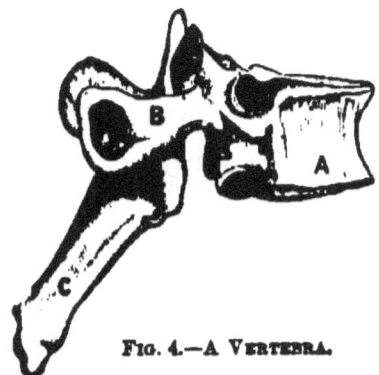

FIG. 4.—A VERTEBRA.

A.—The body of the Vertebra.
B.—Transverse Process.
C.—Spinous Process for the attachment of muscles.

there passes a substance called the spinal cord, about which we shall learn more at a future time.

The vertebræ are attached to one another by strong and very elastic ligaments, and between each pair of them is a soft cushion of cartilage. This cartilage is of much importance. It acts as a cushion and breaks the force of any sudden jar or shock, which otherwise might injure the brain or the spinal column itself. The spinal column is capable of movement to a limited extent. When you lean forward, the front parts of the cartilages, being soft and elastic, are pressed out and made thinner; and when you again take an upright position, they regain their original shape. If, when sitting, you should allow your back to incline forward continually, these cartilages would after awhile lose their elasticity and be unable to regain their proper shape. It is in this way that the deformity of round shoulders is often caused. The spinal column serves as a support for the whole body. It protects the spinal cord, and to it, at different places, are

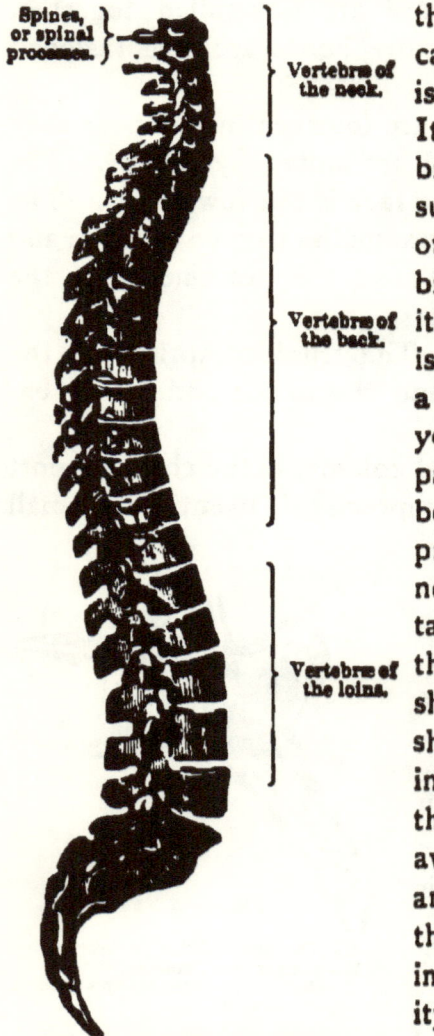

Spines, or spinal processes.

Vertebræ of the neck.

Vertebræ of the back.

Vertebræ of the loins.

FIG. 5.—THE SPINAL COLUMN.

fastened a great many strong muscles which help to keep

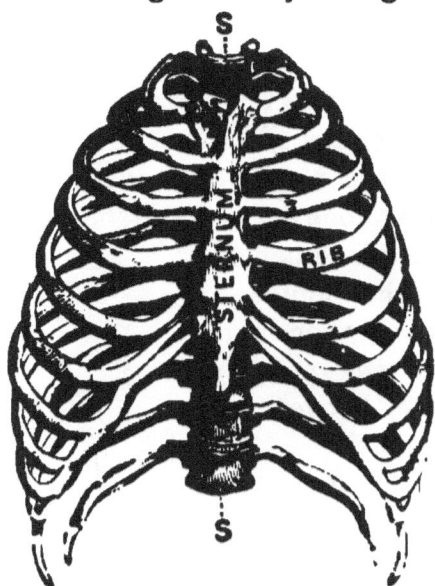

the body erect, or aid in its various movements.

In the trunk there are two cavities, called respectively the *thorax*, or *chest*, and the *abdomen*.

The chest occupies the upper half of the trunk and contains the heart and the lungs. The abdomen occupies the lower half of the trunk and contains the stomach and several other organs. The bones that enclose the chest are the *sternum* or

FIG. 6.—THE CHEST.
S. S.—The spinal column.

breastbone in front, and twelve ribs on each side. The ribs are all joined to the backbone, and most of them to the sternum in front, as shown in Fig. 6. The bones of the chest form a kind of cage for the protection of the important organs that are within it.

The *pelvis* is a cup-shaped basin at the lower part of the abdomen. It is composed chiefly of two large irregular bones called the hip-bones. It serves to contain and sup-

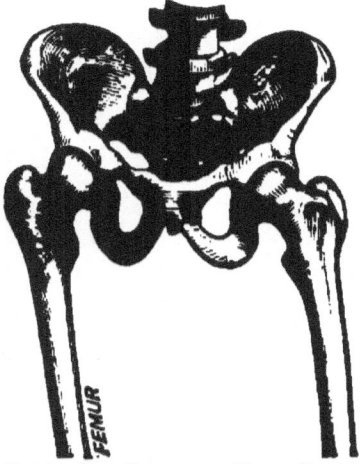

FIG. 7.—THE PELVIS AND THIGH BONES.

port the organs of the abdomen. The pelvis is connected with the backbone, and serves for the attachment of the thigh bones.

15. The Bones of the Extremities.—The upper extremities comprise the shoulders, arms, and hands. In each shoulder there are two bones: the *clavicle* or collar-bone in front, and the *scapula* or shoulder-blade behind. The arm from the shoulder to the elbow consists of one bone called the *humerus*. The part of the arm between the elbow and the wrist is called the forearm and consists of two bones, the *radius* and the *ulna*. The wrist is composed of eight small short bones called the *carpal* or wrist bones. From the wrist to the fingers are five bones called the *metacarpal* bones; and in the fingers are fourteen bones called the *phalanges*, two in the thumb and three in each finger.

FIG. 8.—BONES OF THE SHOULDER, ARM, AND HAND.

Sc.—Scapula.
Cl.—Clavicle.
U.—Ulna.
R.—Radius.
C.—Carpal Bones.
Mc.—Metacarpal Bones.

The lower extremities comprise the legs and feet. The large bone extending from the hip to the knee is called the *femur*, or thigh bone. It is the longest and strongest bone of the body. Extending from the knee to the

FIG. 9.—BONES OF THE LEG AND FOOT.

F.—Femur.
P.—Patella.
Tb.—Tibia.
Fb.—Fibula.
Tr.—Tarsal Bones.
Mt.—Metatarsal Bones.
H.—Phalanges.

ankle are two bones, a large one called the *tibia* and a smaller one called the *fibula*. Resting against and in front of the knee-joint, is a small bone, flat and nearly round, known as the *patella*, or knee-cap. The use of the knee-cap is to protect the joint from injury in case of a blow or a fall. The ankle and heel are made up of seven small bones called *tarsal* bones. The arched shape of the foot gives elasticity to the step, and prevents the jar to the body which would otherwise occur in walking, running, or leaping. The instep and arch of the foot contain five bones called *metatarsal* bones, and the toes are formed of fourteen bones called *phalanges*.

The long bones of the extremities have their ends enlarged. (See figs. 8 and 9.) This is to form the joints and to give more room for the attachment of muscles. These enlarged ends of the bones are composed mostly of cancellous or spongy tissue. This is to give lightness, for if these ends were composed of compact tissue they would be so heavy as to make motion difficult and awkward. The part of the bone between the enlarged portions is called the shaft, and is hollow. It is composed of compact tissue and the hollow space is filled with marrow.

Rules for the Care of the Bones :—

(1) Avoid straining them beyond their strength.

(2) Avoid the habit of stooping or leaning forward.

(3) Avoid tight clothing, which, by compressing the ribs, may cause deformity of the chest. Do not wear ill-fitting shoes, for they will be likely to disfigure the feet.

(4) Beware of the use of tobacco, and shun all alcoholic drinks.

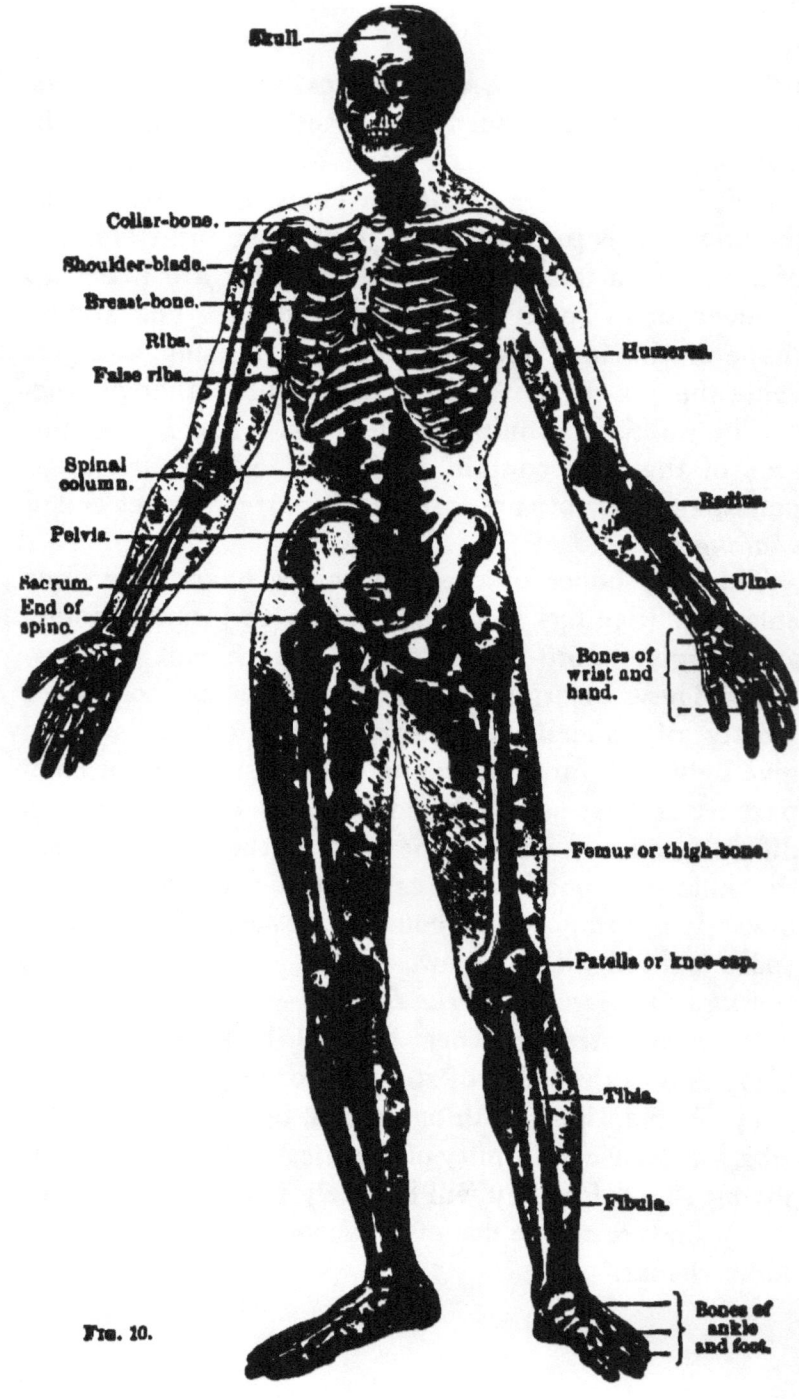

Skull.

Collar-bone.

Shoulder-blade.

Breast-bone.

Ribs.

False ribs.

Humerus.

Spinal column.

Pelvis.

Radius.

Sacrum.

End of spine.

Ulna.

Bones of wrist and hand.

Femur or thigh-bone.

Patella or knee-cap.

Tibia.

Fibula.

Bones of ankle and foot.

Fig. 10.

REVIEW—BONES. OF THE SKELETON.

THE SKULL.

CRANIUM.
- 1 Occipital bone. (Back of head.)
- 2 Parietal bones. (Sides of head.)
- 2 Temporal bones. (Sides of head.)
- 1 Frontal bone. (Forehead.)
- 1 Sphenoid bone. } (Base of skull.)
- 1 Ethmoid bone. }

FACE.
- 2 Malar bones. (Cheek bones.)
- 2 Lachrymal bones. (In orbit of the eye.)
- 2 Nasal bones. (Nose.)
- 2 Inferior turbinated bones.
- 2 Palate bones.
- 1 Vomer. (Part of partition of nose.)
- 2 Superior maxillary bones. (Upper jaw.)
- 1 Inferior maxillary bone. (Lower jaw.)
- 1 Hyoid bone. (At the base of the tongue.)

THE TRUNK.

SPINAL COLUMN.
- 24 Vertebræ.
- 1 Sacrum. } (At the lower end of the
- 1 Coccyx. } spinal column.)
- 2 Os Innominatæ. (Hip-bones.)

CHEST.
- 24 Ribs.
- 1 Sternum. (Breastbone.)

UPPER EXTREMITIES.
- 2 Clavicles. (Collar-bones.)
- 2 Scapulæ. (Shoulder-blades.)
- 2 Humeri. (Upper arms.)
- 2 Radii. } (Forearms.
- 2 Ulnæ. }
- 16 Carpal bones. (Wrists.)
- 10 Metacarpal bones. (Hands.)
- 28 Phalanges. (Fingers.)

LOWER EXTREMITIES.
- 2 Femurs. (Thigh-bones.)
- 2 Tibiæ. } (Legs.)
- 2 Fibulæ. }
- 2 Patellæ. (Knee-caps.)
- 14 Tarsal bones. (Ankles.)
- 10 Metatarsal bones. (Feet.)
- 28 Phalanges. (Toes.)

In the skull .... 22 bones.
In the trunk.............................. 54 bones.
In the extremities........................124 bones.

Total, 200

Note: The teeth are not bones.

CHAPTER III.

THE JOINTS.

16. Definition.—As has already been stated, the bones of the living skeleton are joined one to another. This is accomplished in most cases by the aid of ligaments and cartilages. Any connection of two or more bones forms what is called a joint.

17. Immovable and Movable Joints.—Some joints are incapable of motion, and are called immovable joints. The sutures of the cranium and of the face-bones are examples of this class of joints. All joints that are capable of motion are called movable joints. This class includes

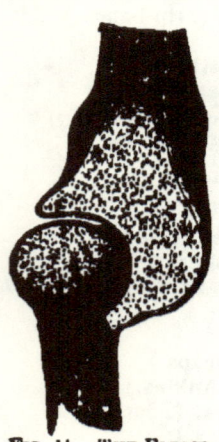

Fig. 11.—The Elbow-Joint.

Section showing it as a hinge joint.

nearly all the joints of the body. In such joints the bones are fastened together by ligaments, and the connecting parts are protected by cartilages.

Around each movable joint there is a delicate membraneous sac, which secretes an extremely viscid substance having much the appearance of the white of an egg. This substance flows, as it is needed, directly into the joint and serves to lubricate it, just as oil lubricates the parts of a machine. This prevents any friction between the bones when they move upon each other at the joint. If it were not for this lubricating fluid, the free motion of the joints would be greatly hindered.

18. Kinds of Joints.—Movable joints are classified according to the kind of motion of which they are capable. In a ball and socket joint the ball-like extremity of one bone is set into a cup-shaped cavity in another. This kind of joint is capable of motion in all directions. The hip-joint and the shoulder-joint are both ball-and-socket joints.

The hinge-joint is one which has a hinge-like motion; that is, it is capable of motion in only two directions, backward and forward. Examples of hinge-joints are the elbow, the knee, and the ankle.

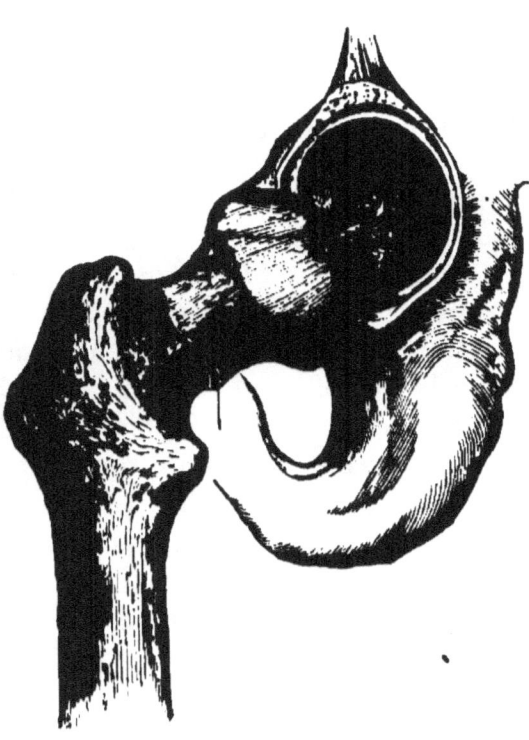

FIG. 12.—THE HIP-JOINT. A TYPICAL BALL AND SOCKET JOINT.

19. Diseases and Injuries of the Joints.—Rheumatism is a disease in which there is inflammation in and around the joints. Exposure to cold and the sudden chilling of the body, are among the exciting causes of this disease, and hence should be avoided whenever possible. Severe inflammation of the joints occurs from various causes, and should always receive careful attention and proper treatment by a physician.

A sprained joint is of common occurrence. It is sometimes a very serious injury, particularly when it happens that the ligaments around the joint are torn or injured. Perfect rest is always necessary to the recovery of a sprained joint. The joint should have the best of care, and it should be remembered that an injury of this kind is often as difficult to heal as a broken bone.

When the end of one of the bones forming a joint is forced out of its proper place by any cause, a dislocation is produced, or as we commonly say, "the bone is out of joint." When this happens to a joint, all motion in it is impossible until the dislocation has been reduced, that is until the bone has been placed in its natural position again.

In injuries of the joints, as well as in injuries of the bones, recovery takes place much sooner in persons who do not indulge in alcoholic drinks than it does in those who are so addicted. It is a well proved fact that alcohol drinkers are slow to recover from any injuries or diseases.

Rules for the Care of the Joints :—

(1) Persons who are predisposed to rheumatism should be doubly careful to guard against colds, or any sudden chilling of the body.

(2) When a joint has been sprained no attempt should be made to use it until it has fully recovered.

(3) When a bone is dislocated, or out of joint, a physician or surgeon should always be called to replace it in its natural position.

CHAPTER IV.

THE MUSCLES.

20. Tissues.—The elements or structures which enter, into and go to make up any organ are called *tissues*. There are many kinds of tissues in the body.

Fibrous tissue consists of long, thread-like substances called fibers, which are very strong and tough. This kind of tissue is found in all parts of the body, binding the various parts and structures together, and serving for both support and protection.

Adipose or fatty tissue consists mainly of fat. It is found in many parts of the body.

Osseous or bony tissue comprises the greater part of the substance of the bones. As has already been stated, it is a very dense, hard tissue, and is either compact or cancellous. (See § 3.)

Cartilaginous tissue is the substance composing the cartilages.

Nerve tissue consists of a thread-like substance called nerve-fiber, united with a peculiar substance made of numerous small bodies known as nerve-cells. This tissue forms the brain, the spinal cord, and the nerves.

21. Muscular Tissue.—The muscles are made up of what is called *muscular* tissue. This tissue consists of bundles of fibers, called muscular fibers, bound together by fibrous tissue. These fibers are elastic and have a very peculiar and wonderful property called contractility ; that is they are capable under certain conditions of

becoming shorter.   In every part of the muscles there
are numerous blood-vessels and nerves.

22. Kinds of Muscles.—The muscles of the body are of
two classes : voluntary muscles and involuntary muscles.

The voluntary muscles are those that are
capable of being put into motion by the will.
They are composed of reddish fibers, and
each muscle is intended to aid in some movement of the body. All the muscles lying on the
outside of the skeleton are voluntary muscles.

The involuntary muscles are
not capable of being put into action by the will.   They are composed of fibers that are paler in
color and of a different shape
from those which compose voluntary muscles.

Fig. 13.—Bun-
dle of Voluntary
Muscular
Fibers.

Involuntary muscular tissue enters into the formation of the internal organs, as the stomach and the intestines.   The heart is an involuntary muscle,
but the muscular fibers of which it is composed are similar in appearance and structure
to those of the voluntary type.

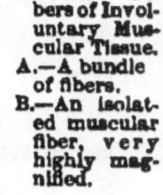

Fig. 14. — Fi-
bers of Invol-
untary Mus-
cular Tissue.
A.—A bundle
of fibers.
B.—An isolat-
ed muscular
fiber, very
highly mag-
nified.

23. Attachment of Muscles.—Voluntary muscles are generally attached at each end to
some part of the body, one end being fastened to a fixed point, the other to a movable point.
Some muscles are attached directly to a bone, but many
are attached to it by means of cords of fibrous tissue
called *tendons*. One end of the tendon is continuous with
the substance of the muscle, the other end blends with

the bone and periosteum. This is illustrated in Fig.
15, below.

24. How Muscles Act.—We have said that muscular tissue possesses the power of contractility. Now when a muscle contracts it becomes shorter and thicker, and its two ends are drawn closer together. This action of a muscle is nicely shown when you bend the elbow. You can see and feel the muscle on the front of the upper arm (the *biceps* muscle) become thicker and shorter as it contracts, thus drawing its two ends closer to each other; and as one end is fixed at the shoulder, the other end which is attached to the forearm, draws the forearm nearer to the shoulder. This contraction of muscular tissue takes place whenever it is subjected to a certain kind of irritation; in life the nerves supply the

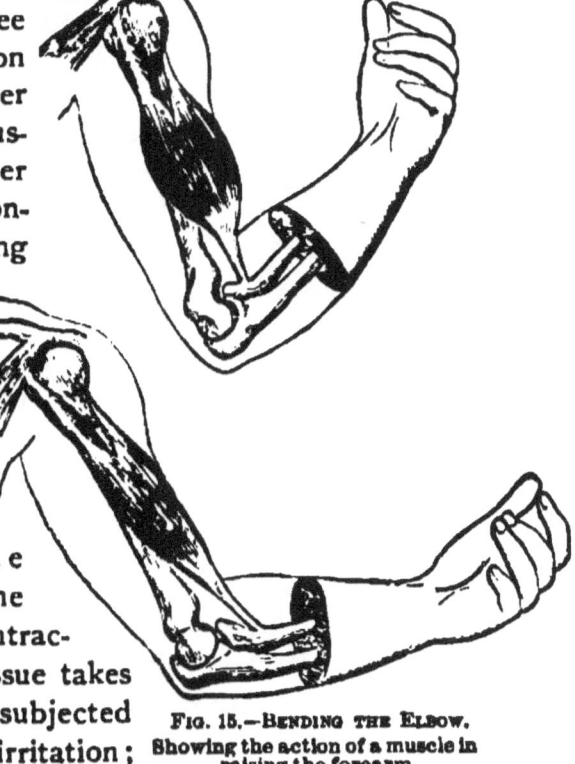

Fig. 15.—Bending the Elbow.
Showing the action of a muscle in raising the forearm.

stimulus or irritation necessary to bring about this contraction. All the voluntary muscles act on the same principle.

25. Form and Size of Muscles.—There are about five hundred muscles in the human body. They vary in shape and size according to the uses to which they are put.

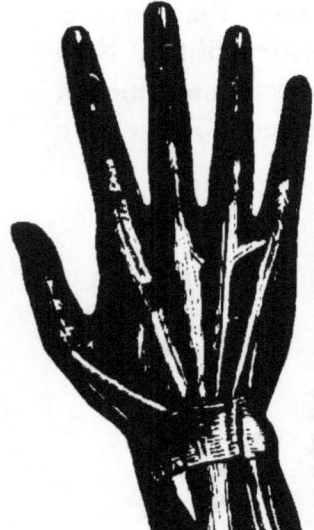

In the extremities the muscles are long and spindle-shaped. In the trunk they are large and broad, flat, and some of them fan-shaped. These muscles serve for protection as well as for motion. Some of the muscles are large and strong, and others are very small.

26. Properties of Muscles.—Muscles have three very important properties :—

FIG. 16.—TENDONS OF THE HAND.

(1) They are elastic. If they be stretched and made longer, they will, when free to act, return to their natural shape.

(2) They have the power of contracting; that is, of becoming shorter. This property has already been noticed in § 24.

(3) They have a peculiar sensibility, which enables us to appreciate weight and to tell whether a body is movable or immovable.

27. Principal Muscles of the Body.—(1) *Muscles of the head and neck.* These are all small muscles. The muscles of the face have two objects to fulfill—one is to give expression to the face, the other is to aid in carrying on the act of chewing, or mastication. The muscles of expression are so placed and attached, that by the contraction of one or more of them, different emotions are manifested in the face. Thus some muscles produce a frown, others a smile; some close the eyelids, others open them; some express laughter and joy, others weeping and sorrow. The muscles of mastication act by moving the lower jaw, raising and lowering it, and giving it its grinding motion. The principal muscle of mastication is called the *masseter* muscle. This is the muscle which elevates the lower jaw with such tremendous force. The muscles of the neck are arranged in layers and are of various shapes and sizes. They give

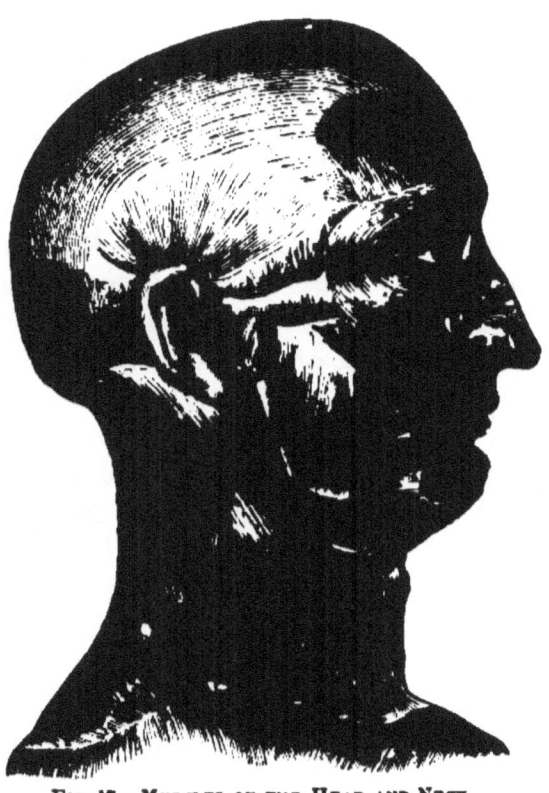

FIG. 17.—MUSCLES OF THE HEAD AND NECK.

to the head its many different movements, and act as a protection to the large nerves and blood-vessels that are situated in the neck.

(2) *Muscles of the trunk.* The muscles of the trunk are most of them large, broad, and flat. Those of the back are arranged in five layers, forming a thick mass of muscles. They are attached to the backbone, and

it is by their action that we are enabled to assume and maintain an upright position. These muscles hold the head in its proper position and give to it some of its movements.

The muscles of the chest are broad, flat, and fan-shaped. They are so attached that by their contraction they aid in the act of breathing. The principal muscle of respiration is called the *diaphragm*. It is a large, flat muscle, separating the two cavities of the trunk. Above it is the chest, below it the abdomen. The walls of the abdominal cavity are formed of broad, flat muscles, which serve to protect its contents.

(3) *Muscles of the extremities.* These muscles are, as a rule, long and spindle-shaped. By their action we are enabled to walk, and to use our hands and arms. They are all very strong, and are so situated and attached that they aid in the performance of a great variety of complex and important movements. Numerous small muscles give to the fingers their various delicate movements.

28. Effects of Alcohol on the Muscles.—Muscular tissue constitutes the principal part of the flesh of the body. It is a delicate living structure. Alcohol has a tendency to destroy all living structures with which it comes in contact, and therefore does only harm to the muscular tissue. In reality it acts as a poison to all forms of life. When alcohol, by which we mean beer, wine, ale, whisky, or any other alcoholic drink, is taken into the system, it mixes with the blood and is carried throughout the body. Alcohol thus comes in direct contact with the delicate muscular tissue, irritating it, and sometimes partially paralyzing it. It interferes with the contracting power of the muscles and prevents their proper development and growth. The continued use of alcohol causes the muscles to become flaccid, weak, and pale, and after a time changes the character of the muscular tissue itself. This change which takes place in the muscular tissue is called fatty degeneration, and consists in the depositing of particles of fat between the muscular fibers. After a while so much fat may be deposited that many of the muscular fibers are crowded out and destroyed, and partially or wholly replaced by fatty tissue. The result of this is that the muscles become weak and crippled, and are totally unable to perform the work that they should.

Many men who drink beer and other alcoholic liquors have large bodies, but this is due to fat and is no sign of health. They appear to be very strong, but this is not the case, for there is no strength in fat. Alcohol never increases muscular power. A man may feel tired and indulge in alcoholic drinks, thinking thus to increase his strength and endurance, but it always happens that he is affected in exactly the opposite way. The alcohol goads him on in his work, but it is forced work, and the entire muscular system suffers by it.

Many trades and occupations are such that they require accuracy and steadiness of muscular action. Persons engaged in such occupations do not dare to indulge in alcoholic drinks. Alcohol acts upon the muscles in such a way as to make both accuracy and steadiness impossible. The muscles become weak and tremulous, and all proper control over their action is lost. They sometimes even reach such an advanced stage of degeneration that they lose their power of concerted motion.

3

If you would see for yourselves this dreadful action of alcohol on the muscular system, notice the tottering walk and the trembling, twitching hands and arms of some habitual drunkard.

To give strength to the muscles we must have food of the right kind and in proper quantities. Alcohol is not a food in any sense of the word, it does not give nourishment or strength to any part of the body, but it does interfere with the nutrition of the body, and thereby takes away its strength.

29. Effects of Tobacco on the Muscles.—It has already been stated that muscular tissue requires for its proper development, good nourishment. The use of tobacco tends to interfere with proper digestion, and therefore with the supplying of proper nourishment to the various tissues. The muscular system is thus made to suffer, and its development is retarded.

The use of tobacco by young and growing persons tends to dwarf the whole body, and consequently the muscular system. Tobacco lessens the muscular power and, like alcohol, prevents all accuracy and steadiness of muscular action. Persons whose occupation demands steady muscles, rarely indulge in it, for it unfits them more or less for their work. Its injurious effects upon boys have become so generally recognized, that in some countries laws have been passed to restrict its use. The use of tobacco is strictly forbidden in the naval and military schools of the United States. The tobacco habit is almost always acquired in youth. The boy who abstains strictly from its use will not want to indulge in it when he becomes a man. But tobacco is harmful not only to young persons; it has its bad effects also on full-grown people.

CHAPTER V.

CARE AND DEVELOPMENT OF THE MUSCLES.

30. Exercise.—To develop the muscles properly, and to promote their growth and health, they must be used. If a muscle is allowed to remain entirely idle, it finally loses its power to make use of the nourishment that is provided, becomes soft and flaccid, and gradually grows smaller and weaker, until at length nearly all of the muscular tissue disappears. Exercise increases the flow of blood to the muscles, and thus promotes their nourishment and stimulates their growth. The effects of exercise are seen in the large, hard, and strong muscles of men who do manual labor, when contrasted with the thin and flabby muscles of professional men who are not accustomed to much exercise. Exercise is essential to the health of the whole body; it increases the circulation and the power of breathing, and stimulates every part of the body to a good healthy growth. Outdoor exercise is the most conducive to health, though indoor exercise has also many good effects. To obtain the greatest advantage from exercise, it should be regular and systematic, and should be taken in proper amounts; then the muscles grow healthy and strong, the joints become flexible, the circulation of the blood is quickened, and the power of endurance is increased.

31. Excessive Exercise.—A proper amount of exercise is beneficial, but too much of it is harmful. At every contraction a muscle loses some of its substance;

that is, a part of its tissue becomes worn out and is destroyed. This tissue however is constantly being renewed by the nourishment supplied to the muscle from the blood. If a muscle be too severely exercised, this wearing out of its tissue takes place faster than new material can be formed, and hence the muscle becomes fatigued and is unable to do its regular amount of work. When a muscle becomes fatigued it takes quite a time for it to regain its normal condition. Exercise should never be continued until it produces fatigue.

32. Indoor Exercises.—The use of gymnastic exercises, especially by students and others who are confined much of the time indoors, is a valuable means of promoting the development of the muscles and the growth and strength of the body. These exercises may be so conducted as to bring into action all the muscles of the body. Many of them may be taken in the schoolroom or at home with most beneficial results. A certain time each day should be devoted to them, and if they are practiced faithfully and systematically, the result will be stronger, healthier, and better developed bodies.

The following is a series of indoor exercises which may be easily practiced either in the home or in the schoolroom. They should be conducted in such a manner that each group of muscles shall receive its proper share of attention and the whole body be developed symmetrically. In most of these exercises dumb-bells are supposed to be used. One-pound bells are heavy enough to begin with. If dumb-bells are not available, practice with the hands tightly closed.

33. Exercises for the Muscles of the Back.—*Exercise I.*—Stand up straight with the chest expanded and the arms out in front of you. Have a dumb-bell in each hand. Now draw first one elbow and then the other quickly back, returning them alternately to their first position. This brings into play the muscles on and between the shoulders.

Fio. 18.—Exercise I.

Exercise II.—Stand erect with the arms hanging down at the sides, and a dumb-bell in each hand. Keeping the backs of the hands turned upward, raise them behind you as far as you can. Repeat this exercise eight or ten times. This will strengthen the muscles on the back of the shoulders.

Fio. 19.—Exercise II.

Exercise III.—Stand erect with a dumb-bell in each hand and the arms stretched out in front of you on a level with your shoulders. Now bring your hands around back of you as far as you can, keeping the arms

Fio. 20.—Exercise III.

straight all the while and on a level with the shoulders ;
then bring them forward again, and so on six to ten
times each day. This exercise
puts the muscles of the shoulder
into action, and will in-
crease their strength.

Exercise IV.—Stand up
straight with your hands
clasped on the back of
your neck. Now lean
forward as far as you
can. Hold the body
in this position till
you count ten, then
slowly rise until you
are again in an erect
position. Do this a
dozen times each day.

Fig. 21.—Exercise IV.

It is good exercise for the muscles of the lower part of
the back. These are the muscles that we use a good
deal in lifting.

34. Chest Exercises.—*Exercise V.*—Stand as erect as
possible. Hold
the chin well up,
and be careful to
have the chest ex-
panded. Raise
your hands high
above your head.
Now without bend-

Fig. 22.—Exercise V.

ing the elbows, lower the hands far out sideways until
they are on a level with the shoulders, then slowly raise

them again, drawing in the breath as you do so.   Do this six or eight times each day.

Exercise VI.—Stand erect with the arms straight out at the sides on a level with the shoulders. Holding the arms straight, bring the dumb-bells together in front of you, keeping them all the time on a level with the shoulders. Do this a dozen times each day.

FIG. 23.—Exercise VI.

Exercise VII.—Stand in the aisle between two desks or tables, with a hand on each. Step back a little, then bend the elbows and lean forward till your chest is on a level with your hands, then slowly rise again. Try this exercise ten times each day. These chest exercises will not only develop the muscles of the chest, but will expand it and increase the breathing capacity.

35. Arm Exercises. — *Exercise VIII.*—Hold the arms full length in front of you with the hands opened wide. Now close the hands tightly, then open them, then close them

FIG. 24.—Exercise VII.

again, and keep on doing this twenty or thirty times
each day. In this way you will put into action the muscles of the forearm that are used
in the act of grasping.

Exercise IX.—Stand erect and
hold the arms straight out in front
of you, having in one hand a
long, round stick. Now twirl
the stick as far as you can, first
one way, then the other. Do this
several times, and then practice in
the same way with the other hand.
In this manner you will promote
the development of the muscles of
the forearm that are used in twist-
ing the hand and wrist.

Exercise X.—Take a stick about
two feet long, and grasp it with the
hands, one at each end. Twist it

Fig. 25.—Exercise IX.

from you with one hand, at the
same time try to twist it from you with
the other. This puts into action the
same muscles as in
the previous exercise.
Try this say eight
times each day.

Exercise XI.—
Stand up straight,
holding your arms
down at your sides.

Fig. 26.—Exercise X.

Draw in your breath,

Fig. 27.—Exercise XI.

expand your chest, and keeping the elbows close to the

body, bend the elbows, first one and then the other, raising the hands to the shoulders, dropping them again to the sides, and so on, say a dozen times each day. This is a good exercise for bringing into action the muscles of the upper arm that are used in bending the elbow. The principal one of these muscles is called the biceps muscle. Find it in the arm above the elbow.

Exercise XII.—Stand up straight and hold your right arm down at your side, having the elbow bent a little. Place your left hand upon your right, and as you raise your right hand press down upon it with your left. Do the same with the other arm. Practice this simple exercise nine or ten times daily.

Fig. 28.—Exercise XII.

It also will bring into action the biceps muscle and give it greater strength.

Exercise XIII.—Stand up straight, while you hold both hands high above your head. Bend the elbows, letting the hands slowly fall to the shoulders, then slowly raise them again. Do this nine or ten times a day. Do it also first with one hand, then with the other. This exercise will strengthen the muscles on the back of the upper arm. These are the muscles which you call into action when straightening the elbow.

Fig. 29.—Exercise XIII.

36. Shoulder Exercises.—*Exercise XIV.*—Stand up straight, with your arms stretched out in front of you, the hands on a level with the waist. Now keep the el-

bows straight, and raise the hands until they are level with the shoulders. Hold them there a little while, and then let them fall slowly to their original position. Practice this exercise nine or ten times each day.

Exercise XV.—Stand up straight,

FIG. 30.—Exercise XIV.

with the arms hanging down at your sides. Now, keeping the arms straight and the chin well up, slowly raise the hands out sideways until they are on a level with the shoulders. (See illustration with Exercise V.) Hold them there a little while, and then let them slowly drop to the sides again. Do this nine or ten times each day.

Exercise XVI.—Stand up straight, with the elbows bent and the hands against the front part of the shoulders. Strike out forcibly, first with the right hand, then the left. Practice this nine or ten times each day.

Exercise XVII.—Take the same position as before, but instead of striking out in front of you, strike upward above

FIG. 31. –Exercise XVI.

the head. Try this exercise as often as the preceding.

37. Exercises to Strengthen the Legs.—*Exercise XVIII.*—Stand up as straight as you can; then slowly bend the knees until your body falls about six inches; now straighten them again.   Try this exercise nine or ten times.   It will bring into action the muscles on the front of the thigh.

Exercise XIX.—Stand up straight, with the heels and toes both touching the floor.   Now slowly lift the heels and stand on your tip-toes, then slowly let your heels drop again. Practice this exercise as often as the others. It will strengthen the muscles which form the calf of the leg.

These few indoor exercises, if rightly practiced, will do much toward promoting the development of the muscles, increasing the strength, and promoting the health of the body.

38. Outdoor Exercise.—Outdoor exercise of every kind is of the greatest importance to health, and must not be neglected.   The various games and sports which bring into action the muscles of every part of the body should always be encouraged.   Walking, running, and bicycling are among the most healthful of recreations. If you would be strong and well and happy do not allow anything to prevent you from taking plenty of good outdoor exercise.

39. Effects of Alcohol on Muscular Development.—You have already learned that alcohol is exceedingly harmful to the muscular tissue, that it weakens it, and causes an unhealthy depositing of fat in it.   The muscles are capable of much training and development, but to train and develop them properly they must always be kept in a healthy condition.   The muscles of alcohol drinkers are not healthy, and cannot be properly developed.   Athletes who are in training for the performance of feats requiring great physical strength or skill realize this fact, and are total abstainers. If they were not careful in this regard they would be unable to train their muscles properly.

Very many persons imagine that beer makes them strong; and not a few have ruined their health, and brought sorrow and poverty into their homes because of this mistaken idea. They began by drinking beer or cider, which they said would not intoxicate but would "tone up the system." But the habit of drinking being once formed, there was soon a craving for stronger liquors which would not be satisfied. Beer does not give strength, it does not act as a healthful tonic to the system. The use of it can lead to no good result : it may lead to infinite harm.

Alcohol, as has already been said, makes the muscles weak. This has often been demonstrated in the following way: A man who is not addicted to the use of alcoholic drinks, is requested to test the strength of his muscles; after he has done so, a small quantity of alcohol is given him, and he tries his strength again; then more alcohol is given, and so on. In all cases it has been shown that after the man has taken the alcohol, his strength has been diminished. He may think that he is stronger, and such is the effect of alcohol that when one becomes addicted to its use he does not seem able to realize that his whole system is constantly being weakened by it.

Alcohol lessens the power of endurance. Soldiers who do not use alcoholic drinks are able to march farther, and endure more hardships, while at the same time they suffer less fatigue, than those who are drinkers. In the recent war in Afghanistan, the British soldiers found that there was no comfort to be derived from beer or ale, but rather weakness and discomfort. They could withstand the heat of the deserts better when they drank nothing but water, and so they carried no alcoholic liquors with them on their marches.

Explorers have frequently related similar experiences; and it has always been found that in difficult journeys, where many hardships are encountered, those persons who are alcohol drinkers are the first to give up to fatigue or to disease. Several years ago an expedition was fitted out to search for Sir John Franklin who, with a company of adventurous explorers, had been lost somewhere in the Arctic seas. The ship was loaded with everything necessary for the comfort of the searching party, and besides food there was a plentiful supply of beer, whisky, and other strong drinks. It was thought that these liquors would help the men to resist the cold. At last the region of snow and ice was reached, and the experiment of fighting the cold with alcohol was begun. But it was soon found that alcohol was only a deceiver, and that the men who did not partake of it were much better able to withstand the rigors of the climate than were those who depended upon its help to "keep the cold out." And, indeed, it has invariably proved true that the drinker of alcohol is the first to succumb to any great extreme of temperature, be it cold or heat.

Persons who drink alcohol are much more liable to disease, and much less likely to recover, than those who do not. Alcohol seems to put the whole system in just such a condition that it is impossible for it to resist disease. Many muscular diseases may be traced directly to indulgence in alcoholic drinks.

REVIEW—THE MUSCLES.

There are two kinds of muscles, voluntary and involuntary. Voluntary muscles act as the will directs; involuntary muscles act independently of the will.

There are about five hundred muscles in the body.

Muscles are elastic; they have the power of contracting; they have a peculiar sensibility.

They are of different shapes—round, flat, spindle-shaped, fan-shaped, etc. They are the organs of motion.

Exercise, when properly conducted, develops and strengthens the muscles. Excessive exercise should be avoided. By systematic indoor exercise one may gain much strength and promote the symmetrical growth of all parts of the body. Almost all kinds of outdoor exercise are beneficial.

Alcohol has a paralyzing effect upon the muscular tissue. Its continued use causes fatty degeneration of the muscles.

It never increases muscular power. It tends to make muscular movements both unsteady and inaccurate.

Alcohol is not a food. It cannot, therefore, increase one's strength. On the contrary, it makes the muscles weak.

It makes the body unable to endure extremes of heat and cold. It makes the system unable to resist disease.

Tobacco also lessens muscular power.

It is especially injurious to young people, hindering the healthy development of their bodies.

Persons who indulge in the use of alcoholic drinks, or who have acquired the habit of using tobacco, are not likely to excel in feats of strength, skill, or endurance.

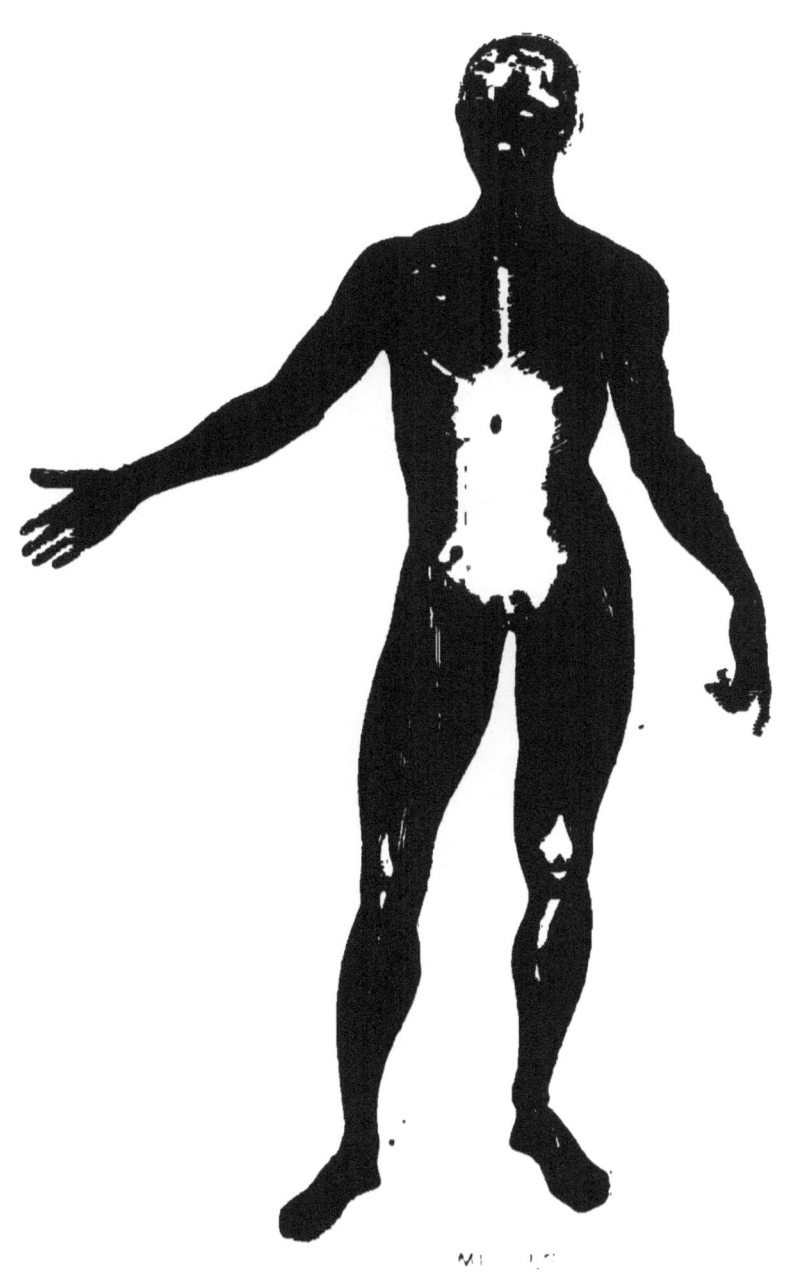

CHAPTER VI.

THE BLOOD.

40. Nutrition of the Body.—We have already observed that the muscles by action become worn out, and must be built up again. This same wearing-out and building-up process is going on all the time, in every organ and tissue of the body. It matters not whether we are asleep or awake, working or resting, the process of destruction and repair is going on, and will continue as long as we live. To repair the tissues that are thus worn out, proper nourishment must be supplied to every part of the body. This nourishment is distributed by the blood, which, by means of its circulation, is carried to every organ, and permeates nearly every tissue.

41. The Blood.—The blood is the nutritive fluid of the body. Its office is to carry nutrition to every tissue in the body. It is the most abundant fluid in the body, comprising about one-twelfth of its entire weight. Thus, a man of the average size has twelve or thirteen pounds of blood. The blood is carried to the different parts of the body through the blood-vessels, and is kept all the time in motion by the organs of circulation. It enters into and flows through every tissue of the body, except the teeth, the hair, and the nails. These obtain their nourishment by a process which we call absorption.

42. Composition of the Blood.—If you should place a drop of blood under a microscope, and examine it, you would find it to be composed of a clear fluid holding in suspension a vast number of small, round, disc-shaped bodies. The clear fluid is called the *plasma*, and the disc-shaped bodies are called *blood corpuscles*.

43. The Plasma.—The plasma is the fluid part of the blood. It is a clear, nearly colorless liquid, and contains in solution the elements required for the nutrition of every tissue in the body. The plasma also serves to dissolve and carry the waste matter from the worn-out tissues to those organs whose work it is to remove such waste from the body. The plasma contains a peculiar element, which, on exposure to the air, causes the blood to become a jelly-like mass. This property will be further explained as we proceed.

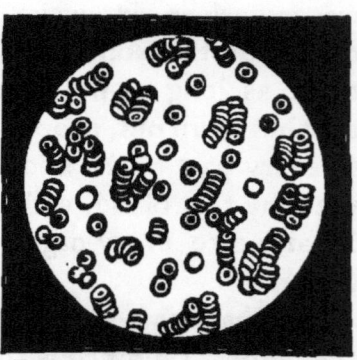

FIG. 32.—RED BLOOD CORPUSCLES. Highly magnified.

44. Blood Corpuscles. — The blood corpuscles constitute about one-half of the entire bulk of the blood. There

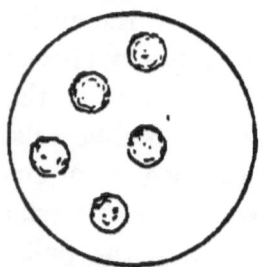

FIG. 33.—WHITE BLOOD CORPUSCLES. As they appear when magnified.

are two kinds of blood corpuscles; these are called the *red* and the *white* corpuscles.

The *red* blood corpuscles are by far the most numerous, there being several hundred of them to one of the white corpuscles. They are the shape of flattened discs, and each measures about $\frac{1}{3500}$ of an inch in diameter, and about $\frac{1}{14000}$ of an inch in thickness. The white corpuscles are larger than the red ones, and instead of being disc-shaped, are globular in form.

45. Uses of the Blood.—Since, with every beat of the heart, every action of the organs, and every motion that is made, some part of the body is worn out, or decomposed—and, since this process goes on constantly—the whole body would soon be destroyed, if it were not that a process of repair and re-formation of tissue is going on at the same time. It is by means of the blood that this repairing process is performed. The blood not only carries to every tissue of the body that form of nourishment which is necessary to the repair of that tissue, but it at the same time absorbs and carries away the worn-out waste matter from the tissues, and deposits it in the proper organs, whence it is removed from the body. The principal organs concerned in this process of removal are the lungs, the kidneys, and the skin.

Oxygen is one of the elements of the air, and is indispensable to all life actions. The red blood corpuscles convey this life-giving oxygen to the various tissues where it fulfills its proper office, stimulating the parts to action and producing a kind of combustion by which the worn-out tissues are decomposed. One of the results of such combustion is the formation of a waste matter called carbonic acid. This carbonic acid is very poisonous, and must be removed from the body. These same red blood corpuscles absorb it and carry it to the lungs, where it is separated from the blood and removed from the body during the acts of breathing.

The *white* corpuscles of the blood are supposed to be concerned in the repair of diseased tissues, and especi-

4

ally to have the power of destroying noxious germs which may have entered the blood, thus rendering the system less liable to disease.

46. Coagulation of the Blood.—When blood is exposed to the air, its liquid form soon changes, and it becomes a soft jelly-like mass called a *clot*. This process is called coagulation, and a clot is coagulated blood. It is caused by a hardening and contraction of the *fibrin* of the blood. The fibrin is one of the elements of the plasma. As the fibrin contracts, it entangles in its net-like meshes the blood corpuscles. This power of the blood to coagulate is of the utmost importance to the human body, preventing great loss of blood from injuries, by plugging up the bleeding vessels.

47. Effects of Alcohol on the Blood.—When alcohol is taken into the stomach it passes directly into the blood, mixes with it, and is carried to all parts of the body. Take a little blood, mix it with alcohol and examine it through a microscope, and you will see that the red blood corpuscles have become smaller and are shrunken. We have just said that one of the great uses of the red blood corpuscles is to carry oxygen to the tissues. When the corpuscles become shrunken by mixing alcohol with the blood, their oxygen-carrying power is lessened, and all the tissues of the body suffer from an insufficient supply of oxygen.

The red blood corpuscles are also concerned in the removal of waste matter from the tissues. When they are shrunken, this power is diminished, and some of the poisonous matter which ought to be removed remains in the system, and the system consequently suffers more or less because of its retention. Especially is this true in regard to carbonic acid.

Alcohol in the blood has also a direct effect upon the nutritive elements of the blood, and interferes with the nourishment of the various tissues. In persons addicted to the use of alcoholic drinks, all the tissues and organs of the body suffer from the want of good and proper nourishment. The consequence is that the proper development of the body is hindered. Alcohol, as we have already said, does not aid in the nutrition of the body in any way, but by its stimulating properties it causes a temporary retention of the waste matters which ought to be carried off by the blood, and thereby sometimes deludes persons into the belief that it relieves hunger or thirst. But this relief is at best only temporary, and results in creating an apparent necessity for further stimulation of the same kind. "Two tablespoonfuls of oatmeal," says Dr. B. W. Richardson, "with one of pease meal, made into a liquid with milk and boiling water, and flavored according to taste with salt or with sugar, forms a drink worth any number of glasses of ale or other alcoholic fluid."

Recent experiments have gone far towards proving that alcohol has such an effect upon the blood as to render it powerless to destroy disease germs. Careful observations have also shown that alcohol has a peculiar influence upon the fibrin of the blood, affecting it variously according to its action upon the water which holds the fibrin in solution. In some instances it combines the water and fibrin in such a way as to destroy the power of coagulation. This explains why drinkers are more liable than others to bleed to death in case of accident ; it explains also why surgical operations upon such persons are so frequently unsuccessful. In other cases, alcohol seems to have exactly the opposite effect upon the fibrin, extracting the water from it and causing coagulation while it is still in the blood-vessels.

48. Effects of Tobacco on the Blood.—Tobacco contains a deadly poison called *nicotine.* So deadly is this poison that one or two drops of it is sufficient to kill a dog or any other small animal. By the constant use of tobacco, this poison is absorbed into the blood, and is carried to the various organs, exercising its poisonous effects on all the tissues. Sometimes severe cases of poisoning have resulted from tobacco juice or powdered tobacco coming in contact with some portion of the body from which the skin had been removed. This poisoning was caused by the deadly nicotine.

Tobacco interferes with the nourishing qualities of the blood, and thus serves to prevent the proper growth and development of the body. Cigarettes are more injurious than any other form of tobacco. They tempt their users to a more extensive indulgence in the habit of smoking, and the practice of inhaling their smoke introduces larger quantities of the nicotine poison into the system. Young men who wish to have strong, healthy bodies should beware of acquiring the cigarette habit— a habit which is fraught with danger, and which at the best can add nothing to their physical strength.

Experiments have shown that the habitual use of tobacco causes the blood corpuscles to become less round, and to lose their power of adherence. The blood becomes thinner, and the general health of the system is impaired.

CHAPTER VII.

THE ORGANS OF CIRCULATION.

49. The Organs of Circulation.—The blood in the body is constantly in motion. This movement of the blood is called the circulation, and is produced and carried on by certain organs called the organs of circulation. These organs are the *heart* and the *blood-vessels*.

There are three kinds of blood-vessels in the body, called respectively, *arteries, capillaries,* and *veins.*

50. The Heart.— The heart is a hollow, pear-shaped, muscular organ, about the size of one's fist. It is situated in the chest cavity, slightly to the left side, between the two lungs. It is held in position by large blood-vessels, which are attached to its base and to the back part of the

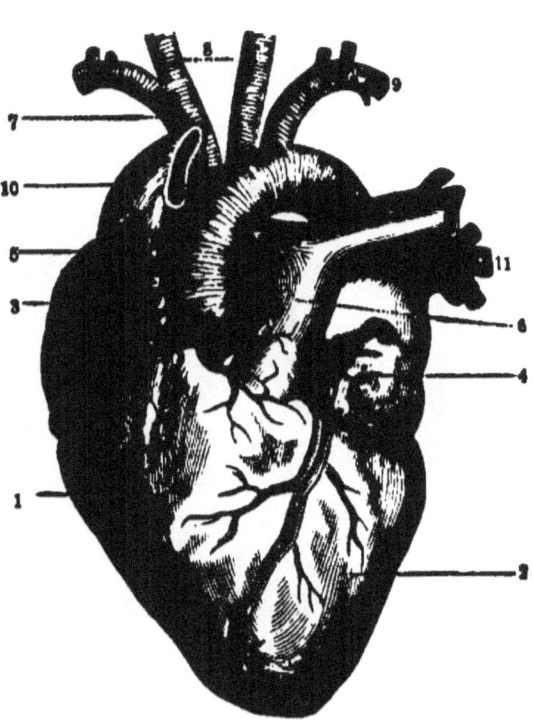

Fig. 34.—The Heart.

1.—Right Ventricle. 6.—Pulmonary Artery.
2.—Left Ventricle. 7, 8, 9.—Large Arteries.
3.—Right Auricle. 10.—Superior Vena Cava.
4.—Left Auricle. 11—Pulmonary Veins.
5.—Aorta

chest. The base of the heart is immovable, but not so the point, or apex.

The heart is surrounded by and loosely enclosed in a strong membrane called the *pericardium*. Between this membrane and the heart there is a small quantity of clear fluid which acts as a lubricator, allowing the heart to move freely without producing any friction.

The heart itself is composed entirely of muscular tissue. It is an exceedingly strong organ, and is capable of contracting with great force. It is also hollow, its interior consisting of four distinct cavities.

51. Cavities of the Heart.—The interior of the heart is divided by a muscular partition into two parts, called the right and the left sides of the heart. The right side of the heart is the part which receives the impure blood from the tissues, and sends it to the lungs to be purified. The left side of the heart receives the purified blood from the lungs, and sends it to the various tissues. Each side of the heart is divided

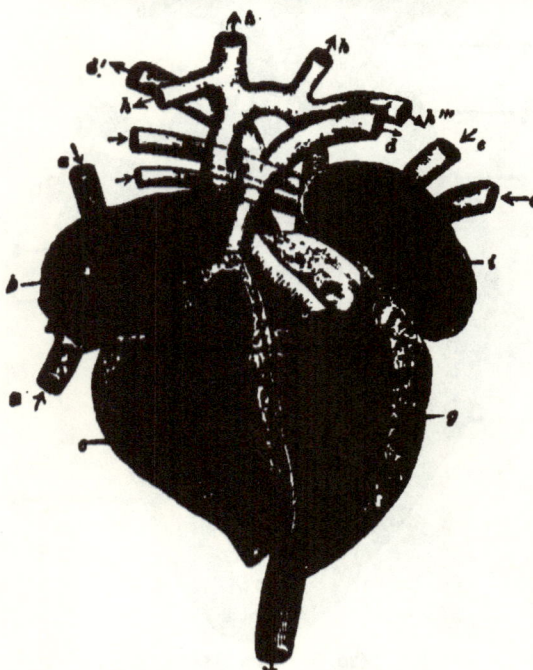

FIG. 35.—CAVITIES OF THE HEART.
b.—Right Auricle.   c.—Right Ventricle.
i.—Left Auricle.   g.—Left Ventricle.
a, d, e, h.—Blood-vessels.

into two cavities, an upper and a lower, thus forming four distinct cavities, two upper ones and two
lower ones. The upper cavities are called *auricles*,
and the lower ones *ventricles*. There are then, a right
and a left auricle, and a right and a left ventricle. The
walls of the ventricles are thick and strong, those of the
auricles are rather thin and not so strong.

52. Valves of the Heart.—The blood must flow only
in one direction in the heart, and this is brought
about by an arrangement of valves at the openings into and from the
cavities of the heart.
Between each auricle
and ventricle is an
orifice supplied with
valves which open
only downward into
the ventricle. These
allow the blood to
flow from the auricle
into the ventricle, but
they close in such a
way that the blood
cannot flow from the
ventricle into the au-

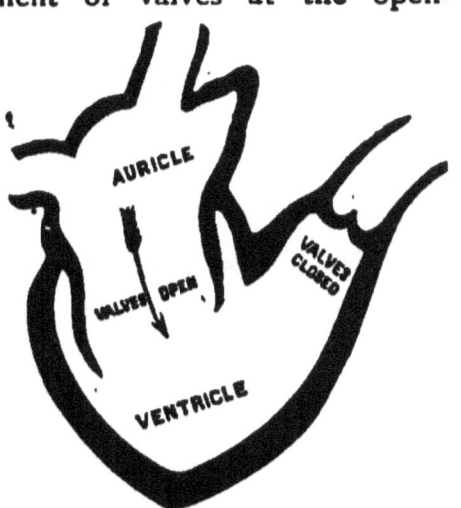

FIG. 36.—VALVES OF ONE SIDE OF THE HEART.
The blood flowing from the auricle.

ricle. Passing out from each ventricle is a large blood-
vessel. At the opening of each of these blood-vessels
there are valves, which allow the blood to flow from
the ventricles into the vessels, but not from the vessels
into the ventricles. Several large blood-vessels open
into the auricles, but these have no valves, as the mild
force of the auricles renders valves unnecessary. It may

thus be seen that the heart has four sets of valves, one set

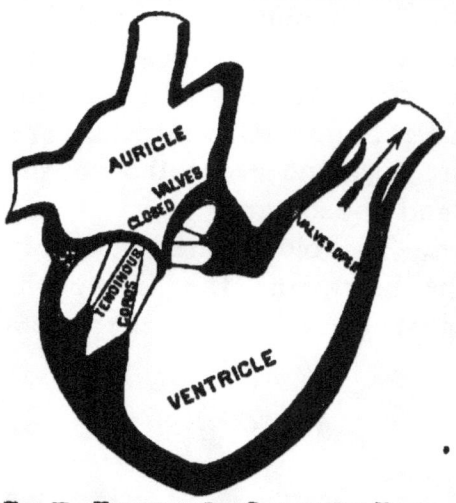

between each auricle and ventricle, and one set at the opening of the blood-vessel leading from each ventricle. These valves are composed of a delicate but strong membrane. Their shape is such that when they are closed no blood can pass through them. Their action will be more fully described later on.

FIG. 87.—VALVES OF ONE SIDE OF THE HEART. The blood flowing from the ventricle..

53. Blood-Vessels Opening into and from the Heart.—Into the right auricle open two large veins, one called the *superior vena cava*, the other the *inferior vena cava*. These pour into the right auricle the blood which has been brought from the tissues. From the right ventricle opens a large blood-vessel called the *pulmonary artery*. Into the left auricle open four blood-vessels called the *pulmonary veins;* and from the left ventricle opens the

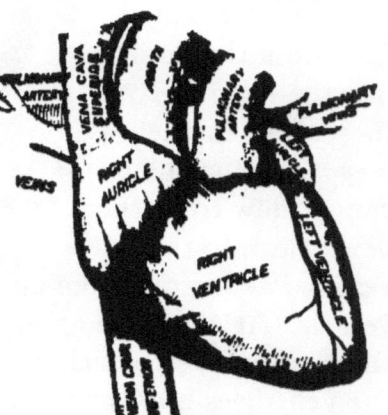

FIG. 88.—BLOOD-VESSELS OPENING INTO THE HEART.

largest blood-vessel in the body, called the *aorta*.

54. The Action of the Heart.—The heart may be called the force-pump which keeps the blood in motion. It has two movements, contraction and relaxation. When the heart contracts, its cavities become smaller, and the blood is forced from them into the blood-vessels. When it relaxes, or regains its proper size, the cavities are again filled with blood, only to be sent out into the blood-vessels again by another contraction. The heart contracts and relaxes, on an average, about seventy-two times a minute.

55. The Sounds of the Heart.—If you should place your ear on the chest of a person, over his heart, you might hear what is called "the heart-beat." That is, with each action of the heart you could hear a sound.

There are two different sounds occurring alternately with each movement of the heart. The first sound, or that which occurs when the heart contracts, is caused principally by the closing of the valves between the auricles and ventricles. The second sound, or that which occurs when the heart begins to relax, is caused by the closing of the valves at the openings of the blood-vessels into the ventricles. These sounds have certain characteristics by which the physician is able to determine the condition of the valves of the heart, and to tell whether one or more of them be diseased or incapable of performing its proper work.

56. Nerves of the Heart.—The heart is supplied with two sets of nerves. One set of nerves causes the heart to beat rapidly, the other set restrains it, making it act slowly, and serving as a check to the first set. Whenever this latter set of nerves loses its power from any reason, the first set is no longer held in check by it, and the heart beats very rapidly, or as we might say, it runs away.

57. The Pulse.—With each contraction of the heart, blood is forced through the arteries. If you place your finger on an artery you can feel it expand every time the blood is forced through it. This is called the *pulse*. The best place to feel the pulse is in the wrist just back of the ball of the thumb.

The average frequency of the pulse is seventy-two to seventy-six times in a minute. It varies in frequency, however, in different persons and under different conditions. Sudden emotions, such as fright, joy, or grief, cause it to beat more rapidly. It beats more rapidly when one is working than when resting; and its frequency is also increased during digestion. Most diseases of the system cause the pulse to become more rapid.

58. Capacity of the Heart.—Each ventricle, at each contraction of the heart, forces into the blood-vessels about six ounces of blood. At this rate all the blood in the body passes through the heart in less than one minute. The aggregate force exerted by the heart in one day's action is immense. It is estimated that the entire amount of blood forced from it, or rather through it, in the course of twenty-four hours is equal to more than 300 barrels.

59. The Arteries.—The arteries are the vessels which convey the blood from the heart to the different parts of the body. They are cylindrical, having firm, elastic walls, formed of muscular and fibrous tissue. The main artery in the body is the aorta. It starts from the left ventricle of the heart, and divides and sub-divides into innumerable branches; as the arteries divide they become smaller and smaller, until finally they are so small as to be invisible to the naked eye.

60. The Capillaries.—The smallest arteries finally terminate in a sort of net-work of exceedingly small and delicate blood-vessels called *cap-illaries.* These capillaries exist in every part of the tissues of the body, and so closely do they lie together, that it is impossible to prick the skin with a needle, without injuring some of them. It is in the capillaries that the blood carries on its work of nourishing and rebuilding the body. It is also in the capillaries that it begins the process of re-

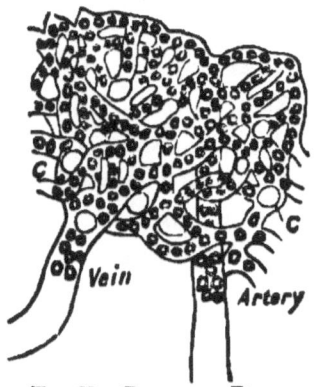

Fio. 39.—CAPILLARY BLOOD-VESSELS (Magnified.)

moving the waste matter from the worn-out portions of the tissues.

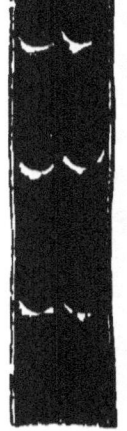

Fio. 40.—VALVES OF THE VEINS.

61. The Veins.—The vessels which carry the blood from the tissues back towards the heart are called veins. The veins begin where the capillaries end, and at their beginning they are exceedingly small. They join one another, growing larger and larger, until finally all the veins of the upper part of the body unite to form one large vein, and those of the lower part of the body unite to form another. These two veins are the *venæ cavæ* (see § 53), and the blood from them, as has already been stated, is poured into the right auricle of the heart. The walls of the veins are thinner and contain less muscular tissue than the walls of the arteries. In the veins there are numerous valves, which are so arranged that the blood is allowed to flow through them only in the direction of the heart. When the veins are empty their walls collapse; but when the arteries are empty their walls retain their original shape.

62. Effects of Alcohol on the Organs of Circulation.—When alcohol is taken into the body, the effect upon the heart is almost instant. The frequency of the heart's action is increased, because the alcohol has a tendency to paralyze to a certain extent that set of nerves whose function it is to hold the heart's action in check. This allows the other set of nerves to have free play, and consequently the heart is inclined to "run away" with itself. This increased action puts more work on the heart; and if it is kept up for some time, the heart becomes weakened on account of being so much over-worked. When the heart works naturally it rests nearly half of the time, but under the stimulating effect of alcohol its period of rest is shortened, causing it, sooner or later, to become exhausted, and its action to become feeble and irregular.

It has already been explained that alcohol interferes with the nutritive powers of the blood. The heart depends on the blood for its nourishment, and consequently when its nourishment is interfered with, it suffers just as any other part of the body would suffer from the same cause. A continued use of alcohol causes a deposit of fat in many of the tissues. This fatty degeneration has a special tendency to attack the heart. Particles of fat are deposited in the heart substance, crowding out and replacing the muscular fibers, and thus weakening the action of the heart-muscle. This condition is most serious. The valves of the heart also often become diseased as a result of the continual use of alcoholic drinks.

Alcohol has also a decidedly harmful effect on the blood-vessels. The walls of the blood-vessels are all supplied with nerves which regulate their size, thus controlling the quantity of blood sent to each part of the body. Alcohol paralyzes these nerves, allowing the blood-vessels to become dilated and enlarged, so that their capacity is increased and too much blood is sent to certain parts. This action of alcohol on the blood-vessels is seen in the flushed face and the red nose of the habitual drinker. The dilatation of the blood-vessels causes their walls to become thinner and weaker, and it occasionally happens that they become so thin and weak as to be unable to withstand the pressure of the blood in them, and they burst. Fatty degeneration of the walls of the blood-vessels often occurs in habitual alcohol drinkers, weakening the walls and interfering with the proper circulation of blood.

63. Effects of Tobacco on the Heart.—The use of tobacco sometimes produces injurious effects upon the organs of circulation. It sometimes acts upon the nerves of the heart in such a way as to modify its action. A peculiar condition of this organ, known as "tobacco heart," is common with persons who are habitual users of this narcotic poison. In such persons the heart's action becomes irregular and weak; very slight influences cause it to beat rapidly, and moderate exercise causes its action to be so forcible as to become troublesomely apparent to them. This results in the disease called palpitation of the heart.

CHAPTER VIII.

THE CIRCULATION OF THE BLOOD.

64. Course of the Circulation. — In the circulation, the blood goes from the heart through the system and then returns again to the heart. Let us trace a portion of blood through its circulation, beginning with the left ventricle. The blood in the left ventricle is forced through the aorta and its branches to all parts of the body. From the arteries the blood passes through the capillaries, then into the veins, and through the venæ cavæ it is emptied into the right auricle of the heart. From the right auricle it passes into the right ventricle, and is then sent through the pulmonary artery to the lungs. From the lungs the blood passes through the pulmonary veins back to the left auricle, then into the left ventricle, the place from which it originally started.

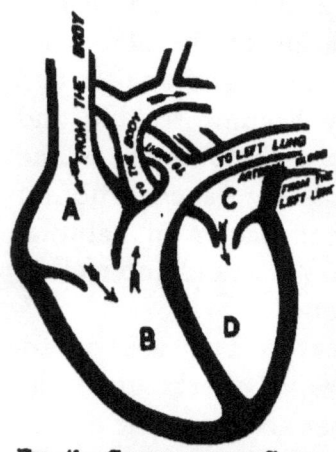

FIG. 41.—COURSE OF THE CIRCULATION THROUGH THE HEART.

65. Color of the Blood.—When the blood starts from the left ventricle it is of a bright red color, and so remains while it is in the arteries. After it circulates in the capillaries it becomes blue in color, and so remains until it is purified in the lungs.   Hence it is generally said that arterial blood is bright red, and venous blood is bluish in color.

The arterial blood is pure and contains much oxygen ; the venous blood is impure, containing much carbonic acid and other waste matter from the tissues.   As this dark, impure blood passes through the lungs it loses its carbonic acid and takes up oxygen in its place, becoming again bright red in color as it returns to the left side of the heart.

66. Proper Exercise and the Circulation. — The heart is a muscle, and is the organ most concerned in carrying on the circulation.   Proper exercise of the body strengthens the heart's action, as it does that of other muscles, and improves the circulation of the blood. It consequently tends to keep the whole body in good condition by aiding in its proper nutrition.   If a person takes but little exercise, his heart soon becomes weakened and unable to endure exertion.   Such a person suffers from shortness of breath, and, if obliged to perform any unusual exercise, he is likely to be troubled with palpitation of the heart.   Proper exercise is really necessary to the proper circulation of the blood.

67. Disorders of the Circulation. — Diseased conditions of different parts of the body modify the proper circulation of the blood.   Any disease of the heart always has this effect.   The valves of the heart are often so diseased that they cannot perform their proper office, and the circulation is, as a consequence, weakened.   Shortness of breath, dropsy, and general exhaustion often result from this obstruction of the circulation.

Heat and cold have a decided influence on the circulation.   Heat stimulates the heart's action, and quickens the circulation.   Extreme cold lowers the heart's action, and enfeebles the circulation.   This explains why in hot weather parts of the body are flushed, and in cold weather are pale and blue.   It is best to avoid exposing the body to extreme heat or extreme cold, and to keep it so clothed as to adapt it to any state of the weather.   Sudden emotions of joy or grief modify the heart's action and the circulation.

68. Hemorrhage. — By hemorrhage is meant a loss of blood from the body.   Nature has its own way of checking bleeding from a wounded blood-vessel. When an artery is cut its walls instantly contract, rendering the vessel smaller and causing the blood to escape more slowly, thus allowing it to coagulate.   By coagulating, the blood clot serves to plug up the divided blood-vessels, and thus checks the bleeding from them. Very often, however, nature is unable of itself to check a severe hemorrhage, and must be assisted.   The best way of checking hemorrhage is by applying firm pres-

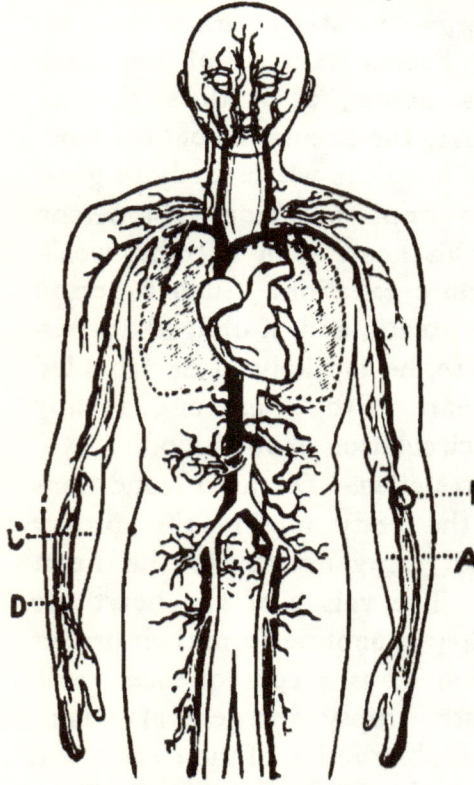

FIG. 42.—INJURED BLOOD-VESSELS

sure on the bleeding vessels. This pressure is to be applied between the bleeding point and the heart, if the
hemorrhage be from an artery; but if it be from a vein,
the pressure is to be applied on the other side of the
bleeding point. Thus in Fig. 42, A represents a bleeding *artery* and B the point where the pressure should
be applied in such a case. C represents a bleeding *vein*
and D the point where pressure should be applied. If
the wound be small, apply pressure directly on it. The
application of cold water or ice to a wound will often
check quite profuse bleeding.

By the application of certain substances called *styptics* we may produce excessive coagulation of the blood,
thus checking the bleeding. The principal styptics
are the persulphate of iron, alum, tincture of iron, and
tannic acid. The styptics should be used only when
it is not possible to apply pressure to the bleeding
vessels.

69. Fainting.—When the circulation becomes so weak
that the amount of blood sent to the head is not sufficient, a person faints, or becomes unconscious for a
greater or less time. The face becomes pale, and the
pulse is weak. To revive a person who is in a faint, lay
him flat on his back, with the head lower than the feet
if possible. This gives the blood a better chance to
flow to the head. Now dash a little cold water into his
face, or apply it to his head. This is usually all that is
necessary to be done. A sufficient quantity of blood
soon flows to the head, and the person recovers.

70. Effects of Alcohol on the Circulation.—The harmful
effects of alcohol upon the heart and the blood-vessels. modifying the heart's action and the condition of

5

the vessels, have already been alluded to. It is easy to understand, therefore, that when it does this, it also necessarily interferes with and hinders the proper circulation of the blood. Too much blood is sent to some of the organs and not enough to others. An excess of blood is sent to the lungs, liver, stomach, and brain, causing congestion of these organs, and interfering with their proper work. The circulation in the skin becomes sluggish, and the skin does not receive sufficient nutrition.

This effect of alcohol on the circulation is easily seen in the face of an habitual drunkard. His nose and cheeks are purplish red in color, and are often covered with unsightly pimples and blotches; his eyes are blood-shot and watery; and his whole face is swollen, giving him the characteristic appearance of an alcohol user.

The arteries of a person addicted to the use of alcoholic liquors become so changed that their walls are extremely weak. When this happens in the arteries of the brain they sometimes burst. In such case death is the immediate result, and the person is said to have died from apoplexy. Sometimes persons who do not use alcohol have apoplexy, but it is much more common with drinkers than with total abstainers.

How to Promote the Healthy Action of the Circulatory Organs :—

Eat wholesome food in proper quantities and at the right time. Take plenty of exercise. Avoid exposing the body to extreme heat or extreme cold. Have a care to adapt the clothing to the state of the weather.

Avoid the use of any drink or other substance that has a tendency to modify the heart's action.

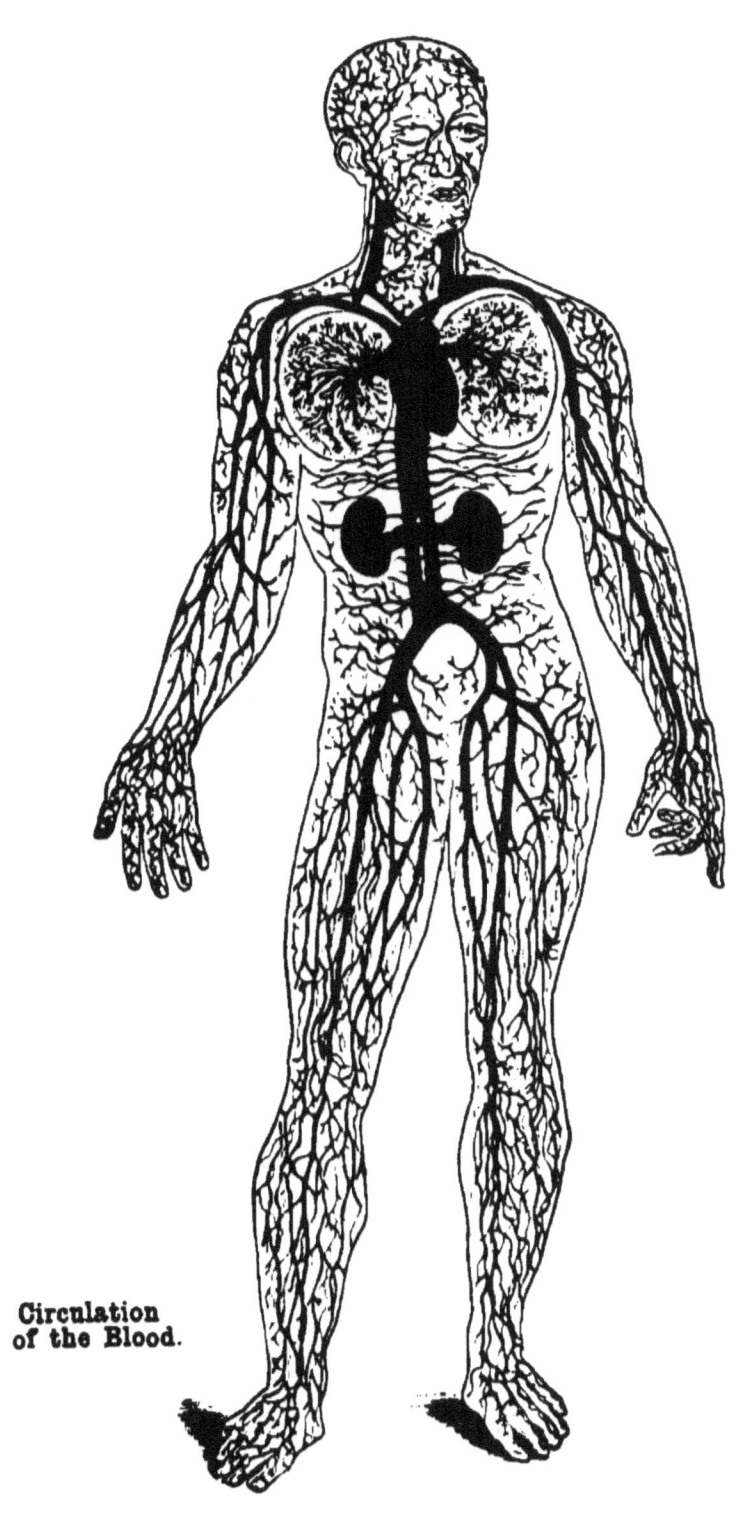

Circulation
of the Blood.

REVIEW—THE BLOOD AND THE CIRCULATION.

The blood is the nutritive fluid of the body. It is composed of a clear fluid called plasma, and of two kinds of corpuscles, red and white.

The blood in the body is all the time in circulation.

The organs of circulation are the heart and the blood-vessels.

The blood-vessels comprise the arteries, veins, and capillaries.

In general, the arteries carry pure blood, the veins carry impure blood. The pulmonary artery, however, carries impure blood, and the pulmonary veins carry pure blood.

The blood is purified in the lungs. Pure blood contains much life-giving oxygen ; impure blood contains much carbonic acid gas and other waste products.

The blood carries to every tissue that form of nourishment which is necessary to its repair or growth. It also carries away the worn out portions of the tissue that are no longer of any use.

The red blood corpuscles carry oxygen to the tissues. The white blood corpuscles aid in destroying noxious germs and in repairing diseased tissues.

When blood is exposed to the air it coagulates. Hemorrhage may be checked by applying strong pressure upon the wounded blood-vessel and elevating the wounded part.

Proper exercise strengthens the heart's action and improves the circulation of the blood.

Violent emotions have a tendency to increase the

rapidity of the circulation. Heat also increases it ; cold retards it. Hence the clothing should be adapted to the temperature of the weather.

Alcohol has a harmful effect upon the red blood corpuscles, and is supposed also to interfere with the white blood corpuscles in the performance of their necessary functions.

Alcohol, by disturbing the nutritive elements of the blood, prevents the proper nourishment of all the tissues. It produces fatty degeneration of the different organs.

Drinkers of alcoholic liquors are less able to survive surgical operations than those who abstain from their use. Alcohol interferes with the coagulation of the blood, and sometimes drinkers bleed to death from what in other persons would be only slight wounds.

Alcohol sometimes causes palpitation of the heart. It causes a dilatation of the blood-vessels, and makes the walls of the veins and arteries thinner and weaker. Its use sometimes induces a predisposition to apoplexy.

The effects of alcohol on the circulation are easily seen in the flushed face of the habitual drunkard.

To have pure blood and a strong, healthy body, one must never indulge in the use of any kind of alcoholic liquor.

Tobacco contains a poison called nicotine. This poison interferes with the blood's action and hinders the proper development of the body.

The smoking of cigarettes is especially harmful, not only to boys, but to men, and the practice of inhaling the smoke is likely, sooner or later, to produce serious results.

CHAPTER IX.

THE ORGANS OF RESPIRATION.

71. Organs of Respiration.—The organs of respiration consist of :—

(1) The *respiratory tract*, or air passages ;

(2) The *lungs;*

(3) Certain muscles which assist in the act of breathing.

The respiratory tract consists of the passages of the nose and mouth, the pharynx, the larynx, and the trachea or windpipe.

72. The Mouth and Nose.—The air passages begin with the mouth and nose. The proper passages for the air to enter in the act of breathing are those through the nose. These passages are lined with a smooth, soft membrane, called *mucous membrane*, the surface of which is increased by the projection into the nasal cavity of peculiarly shaped bones. This mucous membrane is constantly kept moist, thus catching particles of dust from the air as it passes through the nose, and serving also to render the air moist to a certain extent. As the air passes through the nasal passages it becomes slightly warmed.

It is always better to breathe through the nose than through the mouth ; for if one breathes through the mouth, the mucous membrane there is unable properly to purify the air, moisten it, or warm it before it enters the lungs.

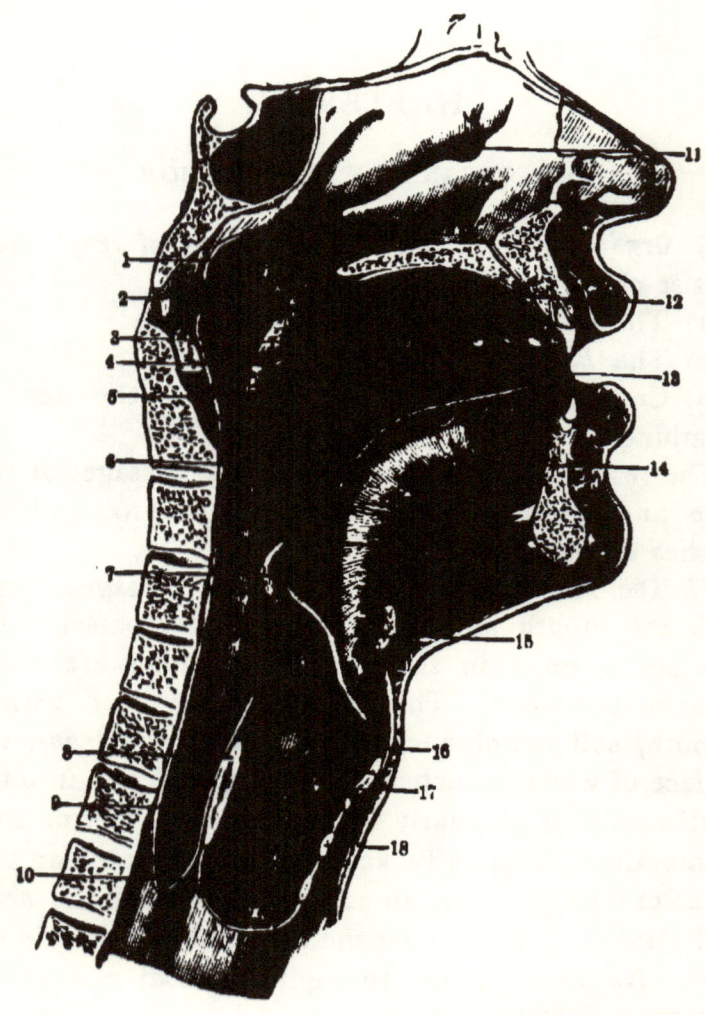

FIG. 43.—SECTIONAL VIEW OF THE UPPER AIR PASSAGES.

1, 2.—Back of Nasal Passage.	8.—Cartilage of Larynx.	14.—Tongue.
3, 4.—Back of Mouth.	9.—Esophagus.	15.—Hyoid Bone.
5.—Tonsil.	10.—Trachea.	16.—Larynx.
6.—Pharynx.	11.—Nose.	17, 18.—Cartilages.
7.—Epiglottis.	12, 13.—Mouth.	

73. The Pharynx.—From the nose and mouth, the air enters the *pharynx*, or as it is commonly called, the throat. The pharynx has two openings at its lower part. One of these is the opening into the *esophagus*, the tube which leads to the stomach, and through which the food passes when it is swallowed ; the other opening leads to the *larynx*, through which the air passes on its way to the lungs.

74. The Larynx.—The larynx is a box-shaped cavity the walls of which are composed of cartilage. It is connected with the pharynx above, and with the trachea or windpipe below. It is lined with mucous membrane. Across its upper opening are stretched two fibrous bands or cords, called the *vocal cords*. These cords are concerned in the production of the voice. Small muscles separate these cords as the air enters on its way toward the lungs, thus making a passage for the air between them. The opening thus formed is called the *glottis*. Just above this opening there is a leaf-like portion of cartilage called the *epiglottis*. During the act of breathing the epiglottis lies in such a position that the passage into the larynx is unobstructed, but when food or drink is being swallowed, the epiglottis shuts down, closing the glottis and preventing the entrance of any foreign substances into the windpipe.

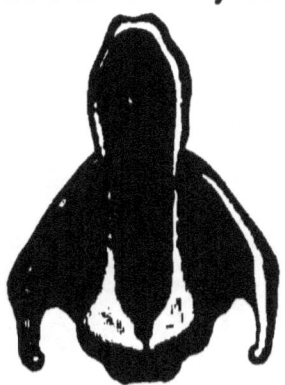

FIG. 44.—THE GLOTTIS.
b b.—Vocal Cords.
A.—Epiglottis.

It is by the action of the vocal cords stretched on each side of the larynx that the various tones of the voice are produced. When the vocal cords have been tightened and drawn closer to each other by the small muscles attached to them, the air, upon being expelled from the lungs, strikes against their edges and causes them to vibrate, thus producing sound. If the cords are stretched tight, the sound will be high; if they hang loose and far apart, a bass tone is produced. The many differences in the quality of the human voice result from differences in the structure of the larynx and in the size and position of the vocal cords. The vocal sound is further modified by the tongue, teeth, lips, and palate, and thus shaped into articulate words.

75. The Trachea.—Beginning at the lower part of the larynx and extending down into the chest is a hollow tube or pipe called the trachea, or windpipe. It is about four inches long and about one inch in diameter. It is lined with mucous membrane and is surrounded by from sixteen to twenty rings of cartilage. The walls of the trachea are composed mostly of fibrous tissue. The rings of cartilage which surround it keep the walls rigid, thus preventing their collapse during the act of breathing.

FIG. 45.—LARYNX, TRACHEA, AND BRONCHIAL TUBES.

After entering the chest the trachea divides into two branches which are called *bronchial tubes*. One of these tubes goes to the right lung, the other to the left.

The trachea and the bronchial tubes are lined with a smooth mucous membrane which is constantly kept moist by a secretion of mucus. This membrane extends with the vessels into all parts of the lungs. Cartilaginous rings also surround the bronchial tubes, and are found even around the small branches of these tubes.

76. The Lungs.—The lungs are two cone-shaped organs situated within the cavity of the chest, one on each side.

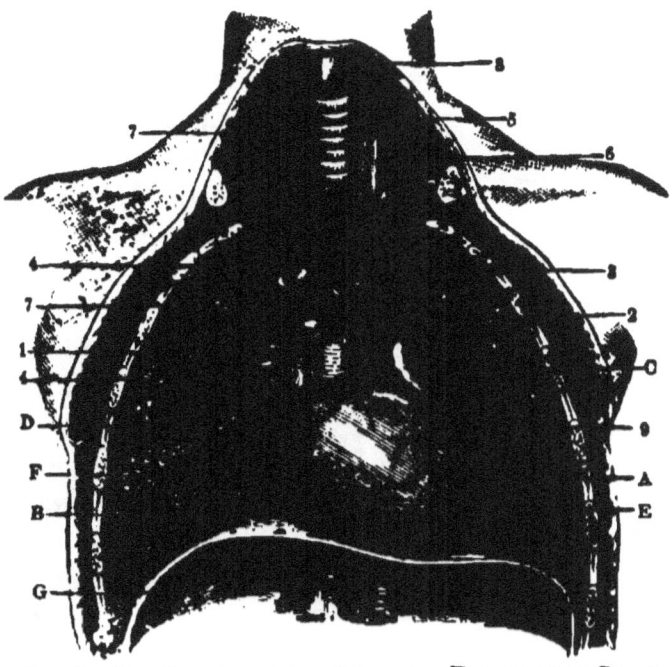

Fig. 46.—The Position of the Lungs and Heart in the Chest.

A, B, C, D.—Heart.	2.—Pulmonary Artery.	6.—Jugular Vein.
E, F.—Lungs.	8.—Aorta.	7.—Windpipe.
G.—Diaphragm.	4.—Superior Vena Cava.	8.—Larynx.
1.—Pulmonary Vein.	5.—Carotid Artery.	9.—Coronary Artery.

Between the two lungs is the heart. Each lung is covered with a smooth membrane, called the *pleura*, which is reflected or turned back upon itself so as to line the chest walls. This membrane secretes a thin fluid, the object of which is to prevent friction between the surface of the lungs and the chest walls during the acts of breathing.

The lungs have a peculiar structure. When the trachea divides into two bronchial tubes, one of these tubes goes to the right lung, and the other to the left. Each tube, after it enters the lungs, divides and sub-divides much like the branches of a tree; the branches become smaller and smaller, and penetrate every part of the lungs. The very smallest of these tubes terminate in minute cavities called lobules. Each of these lobules contains numerous small cells or cavities called air-cells. The walls of the air-cells are very thin and delicate and are formed principally of a net-work of capillary blood-vessels. All the tubes, lobules, and air-cells of the lungs are lined with mucous membrane, the thickness of which varies with the size of the tubes or cells.

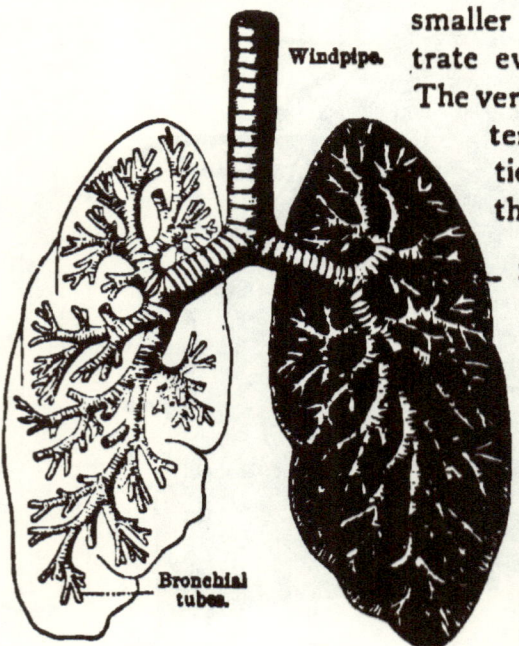

Fig. 47.—Sectional View of the Lungs. Showing how the Bronchial Tubes divide and sub-divide.

77. Muscles of Respiration.—Certain of the muscles aid in the acts of breathing. The most important of these is the muscle called the *diaphragm* (see § 27 [3]). This is a broad, flat muscle which separates the cavity of the chest from that of the abdomen. When at rest, or during the act of expiration, this muscle extends upward into the chest cavity in a vaulted form. When it contracts, the vault is diminished and the capacity of the chest is increased, thus drawing air into the lungs.

The muscles of the chest, which elevate or depress the ribs, also aid in the act of breathing, and are therefore often spoken of as muscles of respiration.

78. Effects of Alcohol on the Organs of Respiration.—No organ, nor system of organs, is exempt from the harmful effects of alcohol when it is introduced into the living body. The delicate mucous membrane which lines the lungs and the whole respiratory tract is particularly susceptible to its destroying influence. This membrane is supplied with blood-vessels and nerves, and contains many small glands, the object of which is to secrete a substance called mucus, by which the membrane is kept moist. When alcohol is taken into the

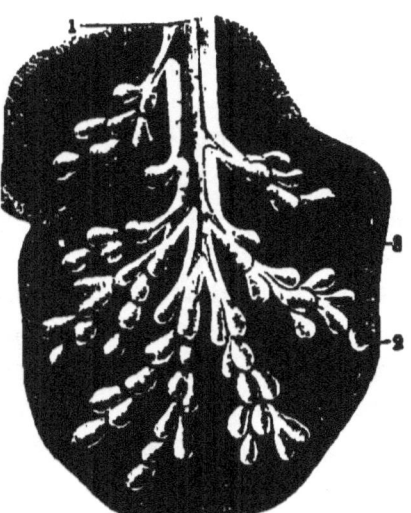

FIG. 48.—A LOBULE OF A LUNG.

1.—Small Bronchial Tube.
2.—Air-Cell.
3.—Lung Tissue.

system, it circulates with the blood and causes the blood-vessels to become dilated. The consequence is that the linings of the air passages are thickened and congested. When the mucous membrane is in this condition the glands are unable to perform their proper work, and the membrane becomes covered with a thick, viscid mucus. This causes a persistent, hacking cough. When the membrane is thus continually congested, respiration is impeded. Colds and lung troubles are easily contracted and are cured only with difficulty.

It is a well recognized fact that persons who are addicted to the use of alcoholic drinks are especially liable to contract pneumonia, and that it is with extreme difficulty that such persons survive an attack of it. Bronchitis, catarrh, and throat troubles are of frequent occurrence among alcohol drinkers, and the continued congestion of the mucous membrane renders recovery very slow.

79. Effects of Tobacco on the Organs of Respiration.—The inhalation of tobacco smoke tends to cause irritation and congestion of the respiratory organs. Many diseases of the mouth and throat are induced or aggravated by the poisonous nicotine which is absorbed by the tissues or brought into direct contact with the delicate and sensitive surface of the mucous membrane which lines the air passages. The throats of many persons are easily irritated by tobacco smoke. This irritation, if continued, causes a redness and soreness of the mucous membrane which lines the larynx and trachea, and frequently results in the disease called " smoker's sore throat." The only cure for this trouble is to give up the use of tobacco altogether. Snuff taking causes many diseases of the nose. That very terrible disease called cancer of the throat, or cancer of the mouth, if not directly caused by the use of tobacco, is certainly aggravated by it.

CHAPTER X.

RESPIRATION.

80. Breathing.—In breathing we draw air into the lungs and then expel it. The act of drawing air into the lungs is called *inspiration;* that of expelling the air from the lungs is called *expiration.*

The chest is really an air-tight box, only communicating with the outer air through the air-passages. Now when the diaphragm and other muscles of respiration contract, the size of the chest cavity is increased and the air rushes into the lungs to fill up the increased amount of space. When the diaphragm and other muscles relax, the

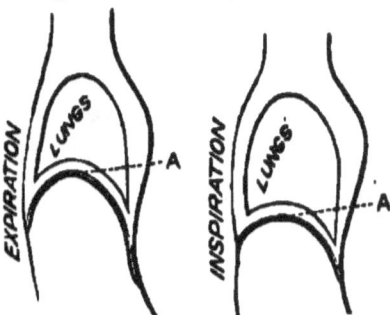

Fig. 49.—Diagram showing the action of the diaphragm when one is breathing.
A. A.—Diaphragm.

tissues of the lungs being elastic, the air is expelled from the lungs, and the chest cavity becomes smaller. It is thus that the act of respiration is performed. A healthy adult breathes from sixteen to twenty times a minute. Exercise and certain diseased conditions increase the rapidity of breathing.

81. Capacity of the Lungs.—The extreme capacity of the lungs, that is the total amount of air they are capable of containing, is about three hundred and thirty cubic inches.   Of this amount, one hundred cubic inches always remains in the lungs and cannot be driven out; another one hundred cubic inches is not expelled during ordinary acts of respiration, but can be expelled by forcible expiration; about twenty cubic inches is taken into the lungs with each natural inspiration and expelled with each expiration; and the remaining one hundred and ten cubic inches is what it is possible to draw into the lungs by forcible inspiration.   From this it will be seen that about two hundred cubic inches of air is contained in the lungs at all times during ordinary respiration, and that only about twenty cubic inches of air is drawn into the lungs and expelled with each breath.

82. Modified Respiration.—Coughing and sneezing are involuntary acts caused by irritation in the air passages of the nose.   In both of these acts there is first a deep inspiration, then a violent, spasmodic expiration.

Hiccoughing is a sudden spasmodic action accompanying the act of inspiration.   It is produced by a quick involuntary contraction of the diaphragm, and with this contraction there is also a closing of the space between the vocal cords.   Hiccoughing is usually the result of some disturbance of the stomach or digestive system.

Laughing and sobbing are modifications of the respiratory act.   Snoring is a peculiar sound sometimes accompanying the acts of respiration during sleep.   It is caused by sleeping with the mouth open and breathing through the nose and mouth at the same time.

83. The Air.—The air which we breathe is a mixture of two gases.   One of these, called *oxygen*, constitutes about one-fifth of the air; the other, called *nitrogen*, constitutes about four-fifths of it.   The oxygen as you have learned, is absolutely essential to all life and to all life actions. The nitrogen does not support life, but serves to dilute the oxygen, thus regulating its supply.

The air also contains a very small quantity of carbonic acid gas. This gas, when pure or nearly so, is very dangerous if taken into the lungs. It is clear and colorless, and is heavier than the air. It is this gas which accumulates in deep wells, old cellars, and mines. It will not support combustion, and hence its presence is easily detected by lowering into any place where it is supposed to exist, a lighted candle or torch. If any considerable quantity of carbonic acid is present the light will be extinguished. This test should always be used before entering a deep well, mine, or any suspected place. Many lives have been lost through failure to take this precaution.

84. The Object of Respiration.—Respiration performs two services in the body, both of which are essential to life. It is the act by which the life-giving oxygen is supplied to the system, while at the same time the poisonous and life-destroying carbonic acid together with various other waste matters, is removed from it.

85. Change in the Blood During Respiration.—When the blood leaves the capillaries and enters the veins it is impure and of a bluish color. It contains much carbonic acid and but little, if any, oxygen. This impure blood goes to the right side of the heart, and from there it is sent to the lungs. In the lungs it circulates through the net-work of capillaries which surrounds the air-cells. Here it comes in close contact with the air that is breathed, and it undergoes a wonderful change. It parts with its carbonic acid and in its place takes up oxygen. It becomes bright red in color and again pure and life-giving, and is therefore ready to be again sent to the tissues.

86. Change in the Air During Respiration.—When the air enters the lungs it is about one-fifth oxygen. When it is expelled from the lungs it has lost much of its oxygen, and has gained much carbonic acid, watery vapor, and other waste matter which it has taken from the blood. It is now loaded with impurities. It is poisonous, and unfit to be again taken into the lungs. The ill effects of this impure air upon the system, when it is again breathed, are especially apparent to persons who remain in close, ill-ventilated rooms or buildings. Such persons suffer with drowsiness and headache, and sometimes with attacks of fainting.

87. Ventilation.—Fresh, pure air at all times is essential to bodily comfort and good health. Air may become impure from many causes. Poisonous gases may be mixed with it; sewer gas is especially to be guarded against; coal gas, which is used for illuminating purposes is very poisonous and dangerous if inhaled; the air rising from decaying substances, foul cellars, or stagnant pools, is impure and unhealthy, and breeds diseases; the foul and poisonous air which has been expelled from the lungs, if breathed again, will cause many distressing symptoms. Ventilation has for its object the removal of impure air, and the supplying of fresh, wholesome air in its place. Proper ventilation should be secured in all rooms and buildings, and its importance cannot be overestimated.

In the summer time, and in climates which permit of it with comfort, ventilation may be secured by having the doors and windows open, thus allowing the fresh air to circulate freely through the house. In stormy and cold weather, however, some other means of ventilation must be supplied. If open fires or grates are used for heating purposes, good ventilation exists, for under such circumstances, the foul and impure air is drawn out of the rooms through the chimneys, and the fresh air enters through the cracks of the doors and windows.

Where open fireplaces are not used, several plans of ventilation may be used, as they all operate on the same principle. Two openings should be in the room— one of them near the floor, through which the fresh air may enter, the other higher up, and connected with a shaft or chimney, which producing a draft, may serve to free the room from the impure air. The size of these openings is to be regulated according to the size of the room. This method of ventilation is sometimes used in schoolrooms and public buildings. It would be well for any one who has charge of an assembly-room of any kind, or of a dwelling house, or who contemplates building, to study carefully the different methods of ventilation. In a book of this kind there is not sufficient space to explain the subject in all its details.

88. Asphyxia.—Asphyxia, or suffocation, results when, from any cause, the necessary supply of oxygen is shut off from the blood. When this happens, carbonic acid accumulates in the blood, bringing it into such a condition that it cannot properly circulate in the body. Asphyxia from drowning, strangling, or any other cause,

6

may be recovered from if the heart still beats, provided that the person be speedily supplied with fresh air from which the blood may obtain the needed oxygen.

89. Artificial Respiration.—The object of artificial respiration is to force fresh air into the lungs, and thus to supply oxygen to the blood. It is, as nearly as possible, an imitation of the natural act of breathing.

Artificial respiration may be performed in the following manner: Lay the person flat on his back with the head a little lower than the shoulders. Then, taking

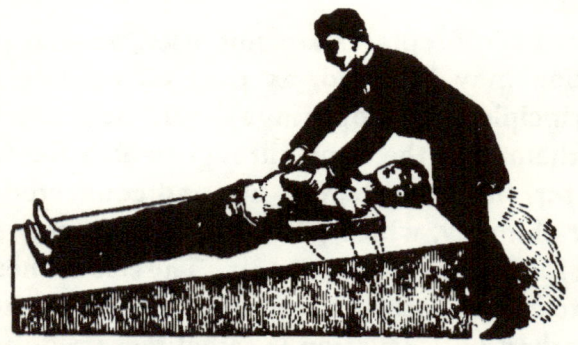

FIG. 50.—METHOD OF PERFORMING ARTIFICIAL RESPIRATION.

hold of the arms above the elbows, bring them above the head as far as possible; hold them there two or three seconds, then bring them down to the sides pressing them firmly against the ribs.

Repeat this operation twelve to sixteen times a minute, and keep it up until the person shows signs of life and can breathe without assistance. When the arms are drawn upwards, the ribs are elevated and the size of the chest cavity is increased, thus tending to form a vacuum. To prevent this vacuum the air rushes in and expands the lungs. When the arms are lowered the chest contracts, and the air in the lungs is driven out, as in natural breathing. Thus both inspiration and expiration are accomplished.

Artificial respiration is always to be used in the resuscitation of asphyxiated persons, and it should be persisted in until it is successful or until all hopes of life are abandoned.

90. Effects of Alcohol on Respiration.—Alcohol modifies the acts of respiration; this modification is due to the effects which it has upon the respiratory organs and about which you have already learned. It lessens the power of removing carbonic acid from the system, and interferes with the absorption of oxygen by the blood. To overcome this, the acts of breathing are increased in frequency.

Alcohol was at one time thought to be beneficial to persons suffering with consumption, but it is now a well recognized fact that its use tends to hasten the progress of that disease. The same may be said to be true with respect to its effects upon other diseases of the lungs.

The breath of a person who has taken alcoholic liquor into his stomach is sure to betray him. This shows that the alcohol has entered into the circulation and that the blood has been freed of a portion of it in the lungs. The air which is breathed out from the drinker's lungs is therefore over-laden with impurities, and should on no account be breathed by another person.

The harmful effects of alcohol upon the heart's action has already been explained. Any injury to the heart of course interferes with the act of breathing, and prevents to a still greater extent the proper purification of the blood in the lungs.

REVIEW—RESPIRATION.

The chief organs of respiration are the nose, the pharynx, the larynx, the trachea, the bronchial tubes, and the lungs.

The larynx is the upper part of the trachea or wind-pipe. It is also the organ of voice.

The trachea is a hollow tube or pipe for the passage of the air to and from the lungs.

The bronchial tubes are divisions of the trachea, one for each lung. They divide and subdivide into numerous branches in the lungs. They terminate in numerous very small cells or cavities.

The lungs are two cone-shaped organs within the cavity of the chest.

The pleura is the covering membrane of the lungs, and also the lining membrane of the chest.

Inspiration is the act of drawing the air into the lungs; expiration is the act of expelling the air from the lungs; respiration is the act of breathing, and is both inspiration and expiration.

The object of respiration is (1) to supply the system with life-giving oxygen, (2) to remove from the system the life-destroying carbonic acid and other waste matters that accumulate in the blood.

The action of the diaphragm and of the muscles which elevate the ribs aids in the process of breathing, or respiration.

Coughing, sneezing, hiccoughing, laughing, and sobbing are various modifications of the act of breathing.

Fresh, pure air is always necessary to bodily comfort and good health.

To promote the action of the respiratory organs and consequently the health of the entire system, one should have a care that the clothing about the chest does not impede the free movement of the ribs and diaphragm in respiration; should habitually sit or stand erect and in such a way as to allow the chest freely to expand in the act of inspiration; should take plenty of good exercise in the open air; should not expose the air passages and throat to extremes of cold or heat; should breathe through the nose and not through the mouth.

Alcohol causes the mucous membrane of the air passages to become thickened and congested. By irritating the throat and lungs, it often produces a troublesome hacking cough.

Alcohol interferes with the acts of respiration and lessens the power of the lungs to remove impurities from the blood. The use of alcohol aggravates and hastens the progress of lung diseases.

Persons addicted to the use of strong drinks are especially liable to pneumonia, bronchitis, and throat troubles.

The breath of a person addicted to drinking alcoholic liquors is over-laden with poisonous impurities.

Alcohol tends to injure the health of the entire system, because it prevents the proper purification of the blood in the lungs, and hence interferes with the nourishment of all the organs.

Tobacco, especially tobacco smoke, irritates and injures the respiratory organs. It causes many diseases of the throat. The continued use of tobacco in any form may finally injure the lungs.

CHAPTER XI.

FOOD AND DRINK.

91. Bodily Nutrition.—It has already been explained that with every movement of the body, and every action of its organs, certain tissues are worn out and decomposed. These worn-out tissues must be replaced by new tissues, in order that the health and strength of the body may be preserved. Hence, every tissue must be constantly supplied with nourishment, in order that its worn-out parts may be again renewed. This nourishment is supplied to the tissues by the blood, and through the blood bodily nutrition is carried on.

Each tissue has the property of taking from the blood only those elements of nutrition which are necessary to supply its own needs. This taking of the elements of nutrition from the blood is called *assimilation*. A proper balance between the wearing out of tissues and their assimilation of nutrition is necessary to health. In children the assimilation exceeds the wearing out of tissues, and thus it is that the body is enabled to grow. In middle age the two processes are about equal, and in old age the wearing out goes on faster than the assimilation, and thus the body gradually grows weaker, and death results, if not from disease, from " old age."

By the discharges from the body, both solid and liquid matter is removed from the system. This loss must be constantly renewed, or the body will die. The loss goes on constantly, whether we are asleep or awake, working or resting. To renew these losses from the system, and to keep the tissues of the body properly nourished, it is necessary to take into our bodies a sufficient quantity of both food and drink.

92. Hunger and Thirst.—When the wearing out of the tissues has proceeded to such an extent that the blood is unable to supply enough nutrition to restore its worn-out parts, a peculiar sensation is felt, which we call *hunger*. Hunger is, in reality, a demand on the part of the system for food with which to supply nutrition to its tissues. The first stage of the feeling of hunger may be said to be appetite, and when food is taken into the stomach this appetite disappears.

Thirst is a demand on the part of the system for water, and this demand must be satisfied, or great suffering will ensue, finally ending in death. A person can live a much longer time without food than without water.

To keep the body in a healthy condition, and enable it to perform its proper work, both food and drink should be taken in such quantities as to satisfy all the needs of the body, supplying it with sufficient nutrition to rebuild the tissues as fast as they are worn out.

93. A Variety of Food is Necessary to Life.—Each tissue of the body requires for its nutrition and development certain food elements. The bones require one class of elements, the muscles another, the fatty tissues still another, and so on with the other tissues. It is plain, therefore, that several food elements are necessary to supply the tissues of the body; and, since different elements exist in different foods, a variety of food is required in order to supply the body with proper and sufficient nourishment.

94. Classification of Food.—All substances containing principles which may be used for nourishing the body are called foods. The principles composing the foods are derived from either the inorganic, the vegetable, or the animal kingdom, and are classified as follows :—

(1) Inorganic principles of food ;

(2) Organic nitrogenized principles of food ;

(3) Organic non-nitrogenized principles of food.

95. Inorganic Principles of Food.—All the tissues and fluids of the body contain more or less inorganic matter ; hence, the inorganic principles of food are essential to the proper nutrition and development of the body. They are found to a greater or less extent in all classes of food, both animal and vegetable, in combination with other principles.

Water is the most important of the inorganic principles of food. It is found in every tissue of the body, without exception, and is absolutely necessary to life. All articles of food contain water; vegetable foods usually contain it in large proportions. Water is the basis of all drinks. In its natural condition it is never absolutely pure; it always contains more or less salts and impurities in solution. The waters of mineral springs are especially rich in salts. Rain-water is more nearly pure than any other. Perfectly pure water may be obtained by distillation.

Another inorganic principle of food which is of vital importance to the body, is *chloride of sodium* or *common salt*. Salt occurs in both animal and vegetable foods. It improves the flavor of food, assists in digestion by exciting and stimulating the flow of the digestive fluids, and meets the demand on the part of the system for a certain kind of nourishment.

Phosphate of lime is an inorganic principle which exists in all forms of vegetable food. This principle serves chiefly to supply substance to the bones, developing and hardening them.

96. Organic Nitrogenized Principles of Food. — These principles constitute all kinds of animal and vegetable food, except the sugars, fats, and starches.

The most important of the nitrogenized foods is *meat* or muscular tissue. Of all the different kinds of meat, beef is the most nutritious. Other meats—as the flesh of birds, fishes, and wild animals, pork, mutton, etc.—are all very nutritious; yet if any one of these be eaten daily, it soon becomes extremely distasteful, and the appetite fails, thus showing a demand on the part of the system for a change of diet. All meat should be cooked, thus rendering it not only more palatable to the taste, but more easily digested.

Next to meat in nutritive value is *albumen*. Albumen occurs as an article of diet principally in the white of eggs. It is an important food, but is of itself incapable of sustaining life. Animals fed on albumen alone, soon die of starvation.

Casein is an organic nitrogenized principle, and is a most important article of diet. It is found chiefly in milk. The various kinds of cheese that are manufactured from milk contain it in great abundance.

Among the organic nitrogenized principles found in vegetable foods, one of the most important is *gluten*. This principle exists in the various grains, being especially

abundant in wheat. It is of the greatest nutritive value
to the system, and experiments have shown that animals may subsist on it as an exclusive article of food
for an indefinite length of time. It seems, indeed, to
supply all the demands of the body for nutrition.
Bread made of gluten is highly nutritious. The presence of gluten makes it possible for bread to be light
and porous.

Several other nitrogenized principles exist in the vegetable foods, the exact properties of which are not yet
fully understood.

97. Organic Non-Nitrogenized Principles of Food.—These
principles comprise the sugars, fats, and starches. They
are all of great importance and are believed to be especially useful in the production and maintenance of
the heat of the body.

Sugar occurs in both animal and vegetable foods.
Honey and sugar of milk are the varieties which are
obtained from the animal kingdom. From the vegetable kingdom two kinds of sugar are obtained. One
of these is called grape sugar, the other cane sugar.
Grape sugar comprises all sugars that exist in fruits.
Apples, pears, grapes, and peaches, all contain sugar.
The chief source of cane sugar is the sugar-cane. It is
derived also from the sap of the sugar-maple and various other substances. All sugars have a sweet taste,
and are soluble in water. Cane sugar is the sweetest,
and also the most soluble.

Fats include all fatty matter and oils. They too exist in both animal and vegetable foods. Fat is found
in all parts of the body, except in the bones, teeth, and
fibrous tissue.

Fat exists in the vegetable kingdom in many fruits and seeds. Cotton-seed oil is obtained from the seeds of the cotton plant; it has now become an important article in the preparation of foods. Olive oil is derived from the fruit of the olive, and is much used as an article of diet. Butter, which is an animal product, is the most important fatty article of diet.

Although fatty foods are of great importance to the proper nutrition of the body, they can not by themselves support life. The amount of fat required as a food varies much in different climates. For people who live in exceedingly cold climates, fats not only form the chief article of diet, but are indispensable to the comfort and health of the body. People who live in warmer countries, and especially in the torrid regions, do not require such foods, and hence use them but sparingly, if at all.

Starch is found chiefly in the cereals—wheat, corn, rye, and barley—in potatoes, peas, beans, and in many roots. It occurs most abundantly in rice. It is a product of the vegetable kingdom only. Starch consists of minute granules. It is insoluble in water, but when boiled in water the granules swell and become transparent, the mixture forming, when cool, a transparent, jelly-like mass. Starch is not assimilated by the system directly as starch, but, by a curious chemical process, it is always converted into grape sugar before entering the blood. Starch also, though an important food, is incapable by itself of supporting life.

98. Drinks.—By drinks we mean substances which are taken into the body for the purpose of quenching thirst. Water is the only substance that will actually quench thirst, and hence it is the foundation of all drinks. Water that is used for drinking purposes should be the purest obtainable. Rain-water is generally the best; well-water, from deep wells, is usually wholesome; and spring-water, if clean, is fairly pure. All water used for drinking purposes should be clear and odorless. If it contains organic impurities, is of a dark color, or has an unpleasant odor, it is unfit to drink, and is likely to give rise to diseases.

Many diseases, such as typhoid fever and others of similar character, have been occasioned by drinking impure water. If the water used for drinking purposes is suspected of being contaminated in any way, it should always be filtered and boiled for quite a length of time before being used. Many epidemics have risen, and many deaths occur every year, on account of neglecting to take this precaution.

The amount of water necessary to the system is from four to five pints daily. This includes the water taken into the body with the food. The quantity of the liquid taken as a drink consequently varies in proportion to the amount of water contained in the food that is eaten. If much soups and milk are taken, less water is required as a drink. For the purpose of quenching thirst, tea, coffee, lemonade, and all other drinks of a similar kind are, as we may say, merely flavored water.

99. Alcoholic Drinks.—Pure alcohol is a clear liquid having a peculiar, penetrating odor and a sharp, acrid taste. It is a poison, and is very fatal to animal life. Immerse any living being in alcohol, and it will almost instantly die.

All alcoholic drinks contain alcohol. Among these

drinks may be classed : hard cider, beer, ale, porter, wine, whisky, brandy, and rum. Alcoholic drinks do not quench the thirst nor benefit one's health in the least. On the other hand, they create an unnatural thirst, and work the greatest injury to the entire system.

Alcoholic drinks are produced by a process called fermentation.* When a substance containing sugar is exposed for a time to the action of warmth and moisture, the sugar in it is decomposed into alcohol and carbonic acid gas. This constitutes fermentation. Old cider is produced by the fermentation of the juice of apples ; ale, beer, and porter, by the fermentation of various grains ; whisky is obtained from corn or rye by distillation ; wines and brandies, from various fruit juices, particularly the juice of the grape. Since corn, barley, rye, and other grains contain much starch and but little sugar, they are first subjected to a process which changes their starch into grape sugar. This sugar is then easily converted into alcohol and carbonic acid by fermentation.

All alcoholic drinks, when taken into the stomach, have a peculiar effect upon the whole system, causing what is known as the alcoholic appetite—that is, they create an unnatural craving for more alcohol. It is this craving which leads so many men to become habitual drunkards. The only safe rule with respect to indulgence in such drinks is this: *Never take the first drink.*

Many people suppose that beer is harmless, that it does not usually cause intoxication, and that it is a wholesome drink which will promote the health and strength of the body. There could be no greater

* See Definitions, page 184.

mistake. In the first place, beer is not a food, and hence it contributes nothing to the nourishment of the various tissues. Habitual beer drinkers are not stronger than other men, but on the contrary are generally weaker. The drinking of beer often causes fatty degeneration of the organs, hence it cannot be said to be harmless. Beer contains alcohol, and hence when drunk in sufficient quantities produces intoxication. The drinking of beer produces the craving for more alcohol, and leads finally to indulgence in stronger drinks, such as whisky and brandy. Even home-made beer that is thought to be so harmless contains enough alcohol to induce this craving for more. The same may be said regarding the nature and action of hard cider.

Whisky contains a very large proportion of alcohol, and no one can claim that it is harmless. Being stronger than beer and cheaper than wine or brandy, it is used more than any other liquor by those who have become confirmed in the habit of drinking. A great deal of that which is sold for whisky is a vile compound of many drugs, containing but very little of the genuine liquor, and it is in the highest degree injurious to those who partake of it.

Brandy when first made is almost as clear as water. Being put into oaken casks it gradually acquires the color of the wood, becoming darker the older it grows. If brandy were always brandy, one might tell its age by observing its color. But very often, in order to give new brandy an appearance of age, burnt sugar and other ingredients are added to it to improve its color, while other drugs of a still more injurious kind are mixed with it to " improve " its taste.

Not only whisky and brandy, but almost all other alcoholic liquors, commonly sold as "pure," are adulterated by admixture with various unwholesome substances. Thus they are made even more injurious to the body than they otherwise would be. It is difficult to obtain wine that is perfectly pure. Of 1,518 samples of wine recently analyzed in the city of Paris, only sixty-five were found to be unmixed with impurities.

100. General Effects of Alcohol on the System.—When alcohol is taken into the stomach, it is quickly absorbed into the circulatory system, where it mixes with the blood in the blood-vessels, and is carried to all parts of the body. Being thus introduced into all of the tissues, it interferes with their proper nutrition, and causes disease. The power of assimilation is weakened, and the discharge of waste matter from the system is hindered or diminished.

Since alcohol hinders rather than aids bodily nutrition, it can in nowise be regarded as a food. Although it may sometimes seem to give temporary relief to thirst, it produces only an unnatural craving for more and more drink of the same kind. It renders the body incapable of withstanding extreme cold or heat.

Alcohol deadens the sensations and blunts the mental faculties. It produces both mental and physical weakness, and if its excessive use is persisted in, it leads its victim to an untimely death.

101. Is Tobacco a Food?—Tobacco is neither a food nor a drink. It is made of the leaves of a tall weed called the tobacco plant. This weed is very extensively cultivated in almost every part of the United States, and in many foreign countries. Although it does not nourish the body or contribute in any way to its real comfort, more money is spent every year for tobacco than for bread.

It is used in a variety of forms, being smoked, chewed, and snuffed. In the preparation of tobacco, especially for chewing purposes, it is sometimes steeped or mixed with various other substances in order to improve its taste or color. Among these substances are salt, soda, molasses, glycerine, and several others that are more harmful. Powdered orris-root is mixed with snuff in order to give it a pleasant aroma.

Tobacco, when first used, causes sickness at the stomach. Nature takes this way of admonishing a person that it is a substance unfit to be admitted into the system. Its effects upon the various organs are similar to those of a narcotic poison.

It produces a waste of saliva. It prevents one from appreciating the delicate flavors of different foods. It hinders digestion. Its immoderate use has frequently induced illness ending in death. Its moderate use is fraught with danger to the health; it not unfrequently causes discomfort to the user and is a source of annoyance to those about him.

The tobacco-habit, when once acquired, can be abandoned only with extreme difficulty. Hence, young men and boys should beware how they fetter themselves with chains from which it will be almost impossible in later years to escape. Thousands of men who acquired the tobacco-habit in youth would gladly escape from its thraldom if they could; but long indulgence in the use of the weed has weakened their will power, and they have not courage to endure the temporary discomforts that would follow any serious effort to abandon it.

CHAPTER XII.

CHEWING AND SWALLOWING.

102. The Digestive Canal.—All food, before it is in a condition to afford nourishment to the tissues, must

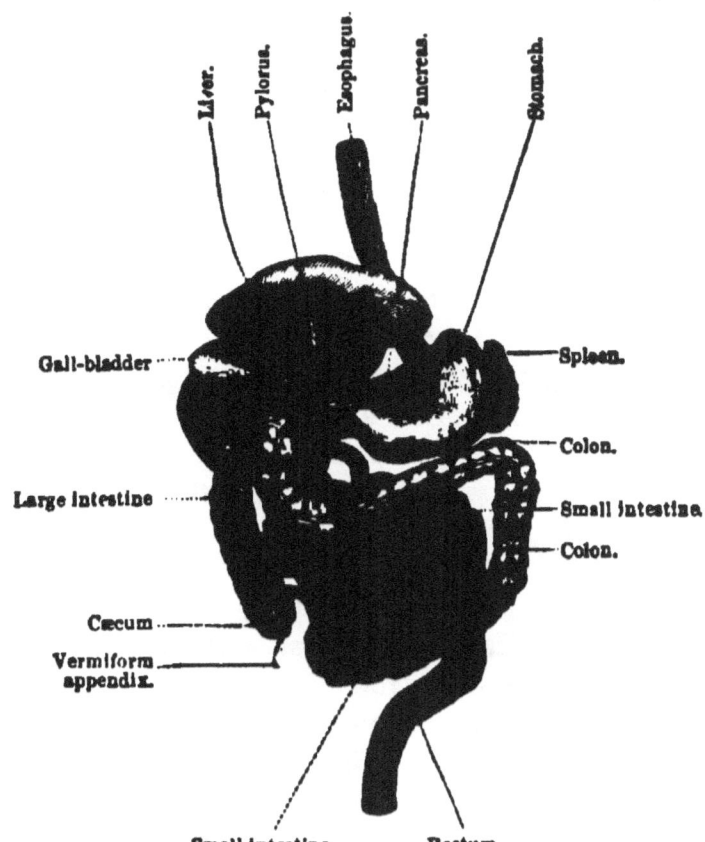

Fig. 51.—The Digestive Canal and other Organs of Digestion.

undergo a certain process in the body, called *digestion*. The passage in which the digestion of the food is performed is the *digestive* or *alimentary canal.* This canal includes the mouth, the esophagus, the stomach, and the intestines. The food first enters the mouth, then passes back into the pharynx, from there through the esophagus into the stomach, and then into the small intestine. Lastly what indigestible matter remains is forced into the large intestine, whence it is expelled from the body.

103. Mastication, or Chewing.—In order that the food may be properly digested it is necessary that, before being swallowed, it should be in a finely divided state and mixed with the secretions of the mouth, so that it can be easily acted upon by the juices of the stomach. This process of dividing the food and mixing it with the secretions of the mouth is called *mastication.* Improper or insufficient mastication is often the cause of a troublesome disease called dyspepsia.

104. The Organs of Mastication.—The organs concerned in the act of mastication are the upper and the lower jaw, the muscles which move the lower jaw, and the tongue, the lips, and the cheeks.

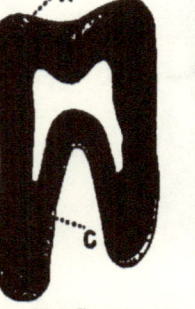

FIG. 58.—SECTION OF A TOOTH. A.—Crown. B.—Neck. C.—Root.

105. Teeth.— Each jaw contains sixteen teeth, making thirty-two in all. Each tooth consists of a crown, a neck, and a root. The crown is that part which is not covered by the gums. It is covered by a white, glistening substance called *enamel.* This enamel is the hardest substance in the human body. It is thickest on the top of the tooth. Its hardness varies in different persons; in some it is so soft that the teeth soon wear away. The greater part of a tooth is com

posed of ivory, and is covered over with a bone-like
structure. The neck of a tooth is the part covered by
the edge of the gum. The root is that part of the tooth

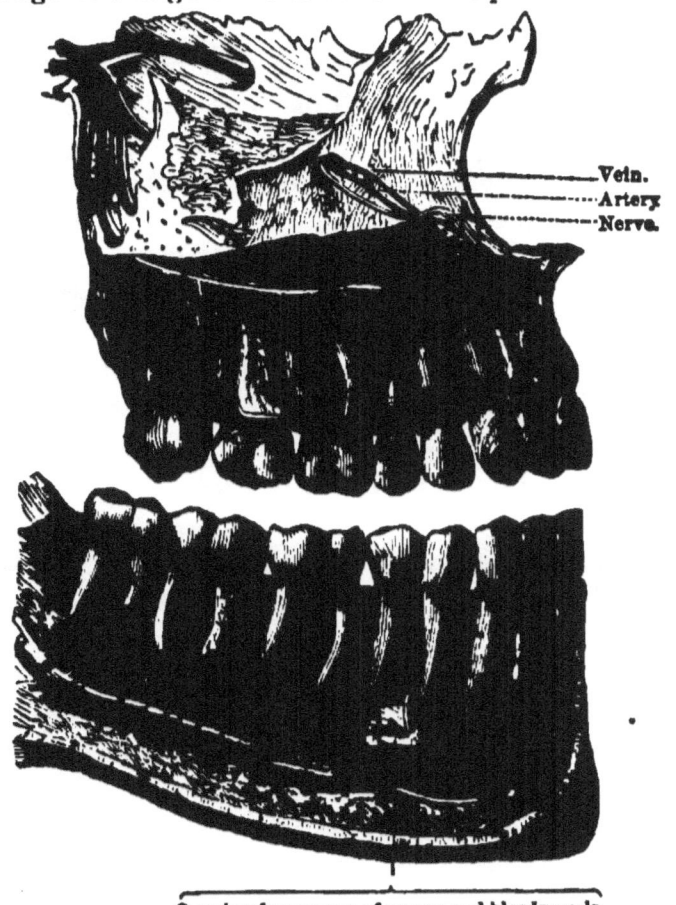

Fig. 53.—THE JAWS AND TEETH.

below the neck, and is surrounded by the bony structure of the jaw.

There are four classes of teeth:—(1) The *incisors;*
(2) the *canines;* (3) the *bicuspids;* (4) the *molars.*

Most people have eight incisors, four canines, eight bicuspids, and twelve molars. The incisors are the sharp front teeth, and are used in cutting the food. The canines are the pointed teeth at the corners of the mouth, and are used for tearing the food. The bicuspids and molars are large, broad teeth, and are used in crushing and grinding the food.

It is very important that the teeth should be kept clean, for injurious substances are likely to collect between or around them and cause them to decay. If the enamel of a tooth is once broken or destroyed, it will not be renewed. One should, therefore, avoid biting very hard substances, or cracking nuts with the teeth. The teeth should be carefully washed every morning and night with water and a soft brush, and particles of food which lodge between them should be carefully removed.

106. The Jaws.—The lower jaw being alone movable, the muscles attached to it act in such a way as to elevate it against the upper one, and at the same time give it a side to side grinding motion.

The tongue, lips, and cheeks all assist in the act of mastication, by moving and keeping the mass of food between the teeth.

107. The Saliva.—The fluid which is mixed with the food during the act of mastication, and which keeps the interior of the mouth moistened, is called the saliva. It is in reality the digestive fluid of the mouth. It is formed and secreted by three pairs of glands called salivary glands. The largest of these glands is called the *parotid gland*, and is situated in front of the lower part of the ear. The next in size is called the *submaxillary gland*,

and is situated below the lower jaw. The smallest is the *sublingual gland*, situated beneath the tongue. All these glands open into the mouth by ducts, and are stimulated to action by the presence of food in the mouth and by the operation of chewing.

108. Object of the Saliva.—The saliva is of the greatest importance in the proper digestion of food. It moistens and softens the food, so that when it enters the stomach the digestive juices there can easily act upon it. It keeps the lining of the mouth moist and pliable. You have learned that before starch can be of use to the system it must be converted into grape sugar. Now the saliva acts upon the starch in the food and changes much of it into sugar, thus putting it in such a condition that it can easily be assimilated by the system.

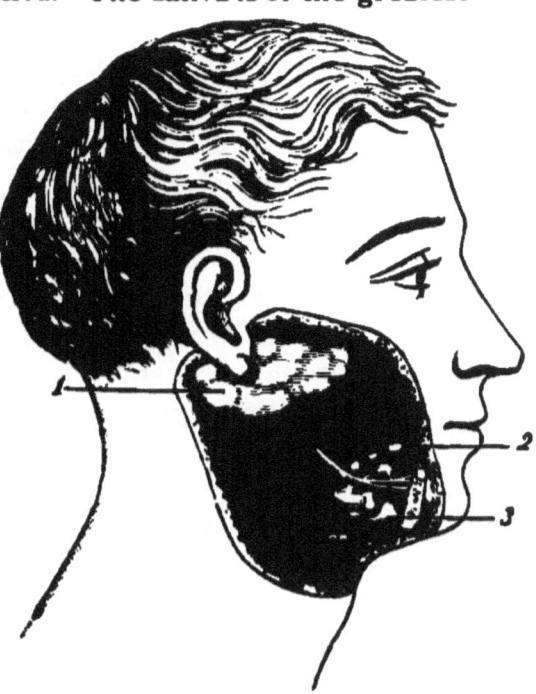

Fig. 51.—The Salivary Glands.
1.—Parotid Gland. 2.—Submaxillary Gland. 3.—Sublingual Gland.

109. Swallowing.—At the back of the mouth is the pharynx, and from the pharynx to the stomach extends a muscular tube or passage, about nine inches in length, called the esophagus. The walls of this tube are composed mostly of muscular tissue, and are lined with soft mucous membrane. In the act of swallowing, the food is forced into the pharynx, then through the esophagus into the stomach. The trachea, or windpipe, also opens into the pharynx, but in swallowing, the little leaf-like carti-lage, called the epiglottis, about which you have already learned, closes this opening so that no particles of food or drink can enter the air passages.

110. Effects of Alcohol on Mastication.—Alcohol, when taken into the system, interferes with the action of many of the glands. By interfering with the salivary glands, it prevents the formation and secretion of a proper amount of saliva. It also changes its quality, and makes it less fit to perform that for which it is intended. As a consequence, many troublesome forms of dyspepsia and indigestion are induced and aggravated. Alcohol also has a parching effect upon the mouth and throat, pro-ducing an unnatural thirst. If sufficient liquid of any kind is drunk to allay this thirst, the digestion of the food. is impaired and the whole body suffers in consequence.

111. Effects of Tobacco on Mastication.—Tobacco over stimulates the action of the salivary glands, causing the saliva to flow oftener and in greater quantities than is natural. This constant over stimulation weakens these glands, and after a while they are unable to secrete a sufficient quantity of saliva for the proper mastica-tion of food. The result is dyspepsia and indigestion. Dryness of the mouth and throat often exists in per-sons who smoke tobacco. This condition is not only troublesome and uncomfortable, but it interferes with proper mastication and swallowing, and in the end is pretty sure to induce disease.

CHAPTER XIII.

DIGESTION IN THE STOMACH.

112. The Stomach.—When food is swallowed, it enters the *stomach*. This organ is a dilated portion of the digestive canal. In an adult it is about thirteen inches long and five inches wide. Its capacity varies in different

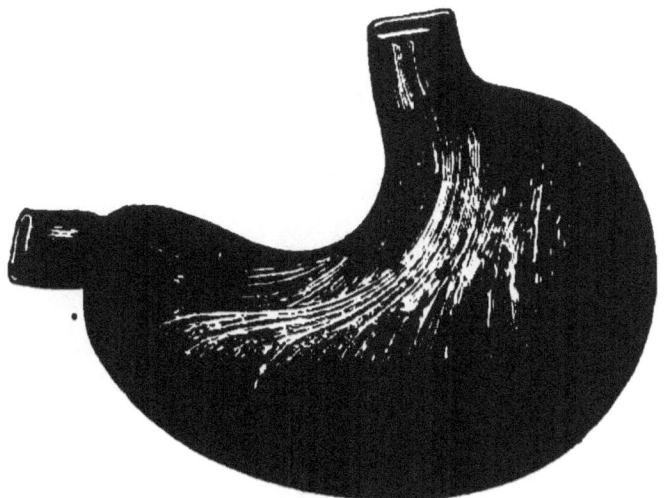

FIG. 55.—THE STOMACH.
Outside view, showing the directions of the muscular fibers.

persons, but on an average it will contain from three to five pints of fluid. It has two openings; one from the esophagus, called the *cardiac orifice*, the other, called the *pylorus*, at the opposite end, where the food passes into the small intestine. The wall of the stomach is composed principally of muscular fibers of the involuntary type. These muscular fibers are arranged in three layers, those of the first running lengthwise of the stomach, those of the second running round it, and those of the third crossing it obliquely.

113. Digestion in the Stomach.—The interior of the stomach is lined with a soft, velvety, mucous membrane. On the surface of this membrane there are vast numbers of very small orifices. These are openings of the ducts

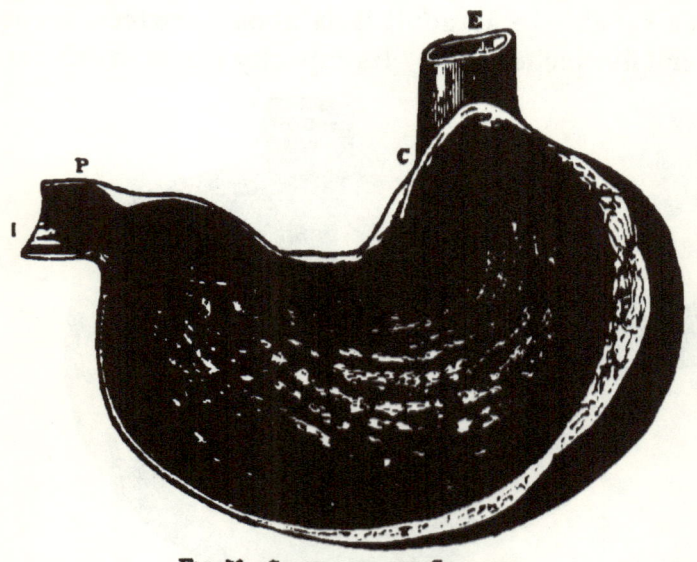

FIG. 56 —SECTION OF THE STOMACH.
E.—Esophagus.   C.—Cardiac Orifice.   P.—Pylorus.   I.—Small Intestine.

from small glands called *peptic glands*. The peptic glands secrete the *gastric juice*, the digestive fluid of the stomach. It is a clear, straw-colored liquid and contains pepsin and hydrochloric acid. Its digestive power is dependent on the presence of these two substances, and if they be removed from it, it becomes useless as a digestive fluid. In the stomach of an adult almost fourteen pints of gastric juice is secreted in the course of each twenty-four hours.

Not all kinds of food are digested in the stomach. The stomach digests only the nitrogenous substances. The fats and starches pass on to the small intestine and are there digested.

Fluids are absorbed into the circulation directly from the stomach.

114. Action of the Stomach.—When the stomach is at rest, its lining membrane is of a pinkish color. When, however, food enters the stomach, this membrane becomes bright-red in color, owing to the increased flow of blood to its blood-vessels, and then the secretion of the gastric juice begins. At the same time the muscular fibers in the walls of the stomach begin slowly to contract and relax, giving the stomach a sort of a motion which causes its contents to roll about its interior. In this way the gastric juice becomes thoroughly mixed with the food. Those portions of the food which become digested are absorbed into the circulation, and when the stomach has digested as much as it can, all that remains is forced into the small intestine where the process of digestion is completed.

115. Time Required for Stomach Digestion.—Different kinds of food, and differently cooked foods, require different lengths of time for their digestion in the stomach. The time varies from one to four hours. The time required for the stomach digestion of an average meal is from two and a half to three hours. Moderate exercise, taken before a meal, aids in facilitating digestion.

116. Care in Eating and Drinking.—We should eat enough, but not too much; and we should eat and drink that which is most conducive to the easy and proper action of the stomach. If the stomach is overloaded the gastric juice is required to do more work than it is able to perform; then, as a result, part of the food is not properly digested and we suffer with indigestion. In this troublesome ailment gas is formed in the stomach, causing colic, diarrhœa, and other disagreeable symptoms.

The temperature within the stomach is about 100°, and at this temperature the gastric juice acts to the best advantage. Now, if ice-water or frozen foods be partaken of, the temperature in the stomach will be reduced and the process of digestion retarded. Digestion is also retarded if extremely hot food or drink is indulged in. Care should consequently be taken to avoid very hot or very cold foods and drinks.

Regular eating is necessary to good digestion. The stomach, like other organs of the body, requires a certain length of time to rest. When one eats too often, that is, between meals and at all hours of the day, the stomach is kept busy all the time, till at last it gives out and is unable to perform its proper functions. It is in this way that various aggravating and painful diseases of the digestive organs are frequently produced.

117. Effects of Alcohol on the Stomach.—When alcohol is taken into the stomach, it acts as an irritant to the mucous lining of that organ, causing it to become congested, and producing an unhealthy secretion of mucus which, being thick and viscid, covers over the mucous membrane, preventing the proper secretion of gastric juice and consequently interfering with digestion.

The gastric juice, as we have already stated, contains

a very important element called pepsin. Without this element it would be of but little use in the process of digestion. Now, if you add alcohol to a solution containing pepsin, it acts upon this solution in such a way as to render the pepsin inert. It acts in a similar way on the gastric juice when mixed with it in the stomach. It thus interferes with digestion, and if the quantity of alcohol taken into the stomach be considerable, the process of digestion is stopped until it has been removed. Very often the presence of alcohol in the stomach becomes so offensive that nature removes it from the system by inducing vomiting.

Persons addicted to the use of alcoholic drinks usually have an offensive breath and a coated tongue. They suffer from loss of appetite, and are tormented with unnatural thirst. These symptoms all denote a disordered digestive system.

Various diseases of the stomach are caused by the continued use of alcoholic drinks. When the lining membrane of the stomach is constantly irritated, it becomes permanently congested, and causes sour stomach, heartburn, nausea, and vomiting. Continued interference with the secretion of gastric juice and with the proper action of the stomach, after awhile results in incurable dyspepsia.

118. Effects of Tobacco on the Stomach.—The use of tobacco very commonly causes indigestion. All tobacco users, especially chewers, are great spitters, and in this way they waste much saliva. Now if food enters the stomach unmixed with a sufficient quantity of saliva, it cannot be easily digested.

Tobacco users have usually a coated tongue, foul

breath, and dry mouth and throat. These are all signs of a more or less disordered state of the digestive organs.

119. Diseases of the Stomach, and Diseases Caused by Unwholesome Food.—Dyspepsia is a common disease. In this disease the food is not properly digested, and, as a consequence, the whole system suffers. This disease is usually accompanied by pain, discomfort, and loss of appetite. The principal causes of dyspepsia are: the use of alcohol or tobacco, irregular eating, overeating, and indulgence in rich articles of food or food too highly seasoned.

Cancer of the stomach is an incurable disease, resulting in a short time in death. This disease, though often existing in persons who do not use alcohol, is especially likely to occur in those who are hard drinkers.

Very many diseases are the direct result of eating unwholesome food. Pork is often infested with minute parasites called *trichinæ*, which, when taken into the stomach, increase rapidly in numbers and penetrate to various parts of the body, causing severe illness and death. Pork chops, ham, and bacon should, therefore, always be thoroughly cooked before being eaten.

Decayed fruits, mouldy bread, sour milk, meat that has begun to decompose, all these, if eaten, are liable to produce disease. The milk of unhealthy cows frequently contains germs which communicate the most dangerous diseases to those who partake of it. Any noxious germs contained in milk may be destroyed by boiling it. If this precaution were oftener taken, much of the sickness prevalent among children might be avoided.

CHAPTER XIV.

DIGESTION IN THE INTESTINES.

120. Intestinal Digestion.—When the food enters the stomach, some of it, as you have learned, is there digested, and the remainder is forced into the small intestine. Before leaving the stomach, however, the food is reduced to a grayish, semi-liquid mass called *chyme*. When this chyme enters the small intestine it is there thoroughly mixed with the *pancreatic juice*, the *bile*, and the *intestinal juice*—all of which are digestive fluids. There the process of digestion is completed. There the sugars, fats, and starches are all changed and prepared for absorption into the circulation.

121. The Small Intestine. —The small intestine is that portion of the digestive canal between the stomach and the large intestine. It is a tube about twenty feet in length. Its walls are

Fig. 57.—Section of Small Intestine. (Magnified.)

formed of muscular tissue, like that of the stomach, and it is lined with mucous membrane. This membrane contains many glands which secrete the intestinal

juice. On the surface of the membrane are numerous
hair-like projections called villi, the function of which is

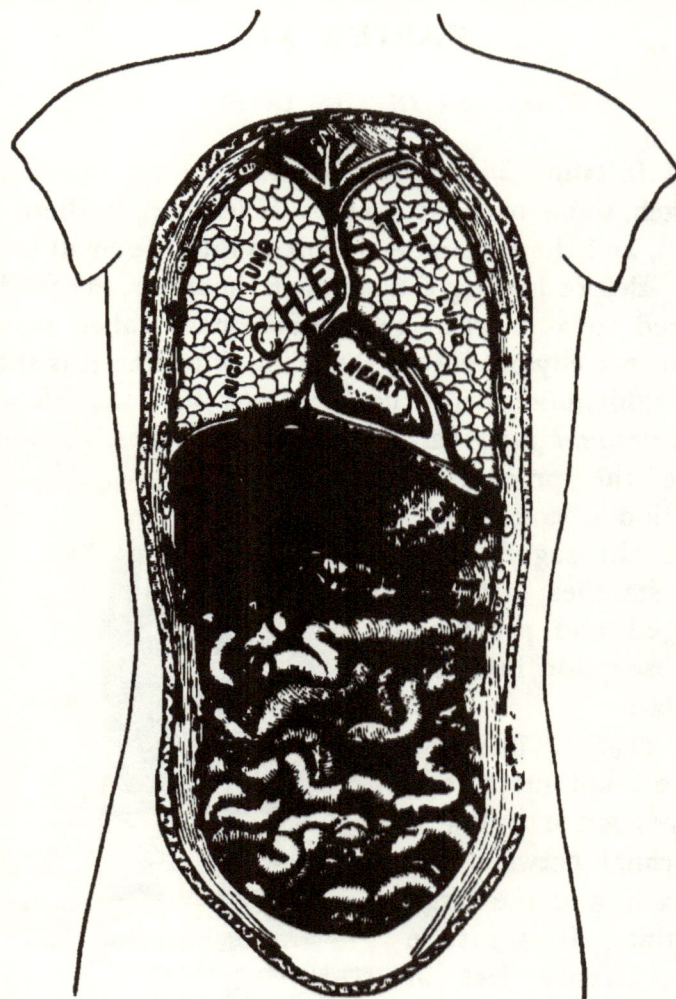

FIG. 58.—RELATIVE POSITION OF THE INTERNAL ORGANS.

to absorb or suck up the digested food, and transfer it
to the circulatory system.

122. The Duodenum.—As the small intestine extends from the stomach, the first eight or ten inches of it is called the *duodenum*. Into this portion of the intestine open two ducts or tubes, one from the *pancreas*, the other from the *gall-bladder*. Through these canals the bile and the pancreatic juice are poured into the intestine where they are mixed with the food. With the aid of the intestinal juice they complete the process of digestion.

123. The Liver.—The liver is the largest gland in the body. It is situated in the right side of the body,

FIG. 59.—THE LIVER.

just below the diaphragm. Its weight in an adult is about four pounds. Connected with it is a small sac, called the gall-bladder, from which a duct or tube proceeds into the duodenum. The liver secretes bile, which is stored up in the gall-bladder and then emptied into the small intestine.

124. The Bile.—The bile is a viscid, golden-brown liquid, which is discharged from the gall-bladder into the duodenum. It is a digestive fluid. When it enters the small intestine it mixes with the chyme, or undigested food, and aids in its digestion. Its chief use is probably to help digest the fats. If the supply of bile be shut off from the intestine, as sometimes occurs in certain diseased conditions of the liver, the constituents of the bile enter the blood, and cause jaundice. In such a case the proper nutrition of the body is impeded, and the general health is impaired.

125. The Pancreas.— The pancreas is a gland about six inches in length, situated behind the stomach. It

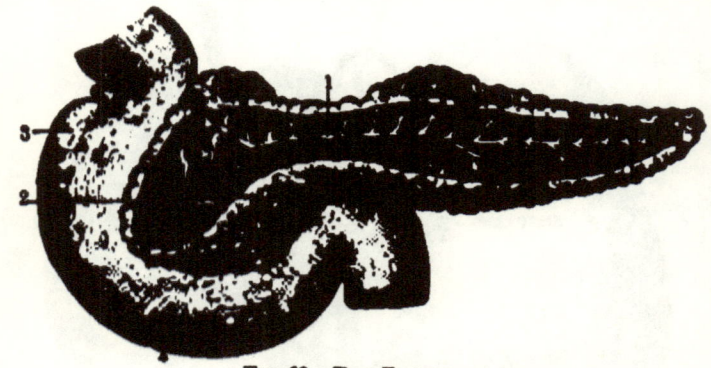

FIG. 60.—THE PANCREAS.
1, 2.—Duct of Pancreas.   3.—Duodenum.

communicates by a duct with the duodenum. It secretes a digestive fluid called the pancreatic juice. This fluid is of great importance in the digestion of food in the small intestine.

The chyme which passes undigested from the stomach contains, as we have already observed, the starches, sugars, and fats which were not acted upon by the gastric juice. These substances now come in contact with the bile and the pancreatic juice. The pancreatic juice acts upon the starch, changing it to grape-sugar. It also changes cane-sugar to grape-sugar; and it acts upon the fats, breaking up the fat globules, and forming a creamy mass, which is capable of being absorbed into the system through the proper channels.

126. Effects of Alcohol on the Liver.—When alcohol is taken internally, it interferes with the action of the digestive fluids, not only in the stomach, but in the small intestine. On the liver especially, alcohol has an injurious and very decided effect, often producing fatty degeneration and other ailments and derangements in this, the largest gland in the body. When this happens, the proper functions of the liver are disturbed, and the secretion of bile is lessened.

One of the most common diseases of the liver, in persons addicted to the use of alcohol, results from the deposit of fibrous tissue in that organ. The fibrous tissue replaces the liver substance, causing the liver to become small and shrunken, hardened, and covered with small elevations, which have given it the name of "hob-nailed liver." This disease of the liver is most serious, often interfering with its functions to such an extent as to cause death.

127. Absorption.—By absorption is meant the process by which digested matters are taken into the blood. During the process of digestion, as has already been explained, certain portions of the food become liquefied, while the fats are converted into a creamy mass, or emulsion. In this way the absorption of the food into the circulatory system is made possible. Two kinds of vessels are concerned in the process of absorption, namely, blood-vessels and lacteals. The liquefied foods are absorbed principally by the blood-vessels, and the emulsified foods by the lacteals.

128. Absorption by Blood-Vessels.—A considerable portion of the food is absorbed through the capillaries and the small veins that are distributed through the lining membranes of the stomach and intestine.   Carefully conducted experiments have demonstrated that soluble and liquid substances pass through the delicate walls of the small blood-vessels, and mix directly with the blood.   This is the way in which absorption in the stomach takes place.   Substances which are liquefied and in condition to mix with the blood are taken into the minute capillaries and veins, and by them soon conveyed into the general circulation.

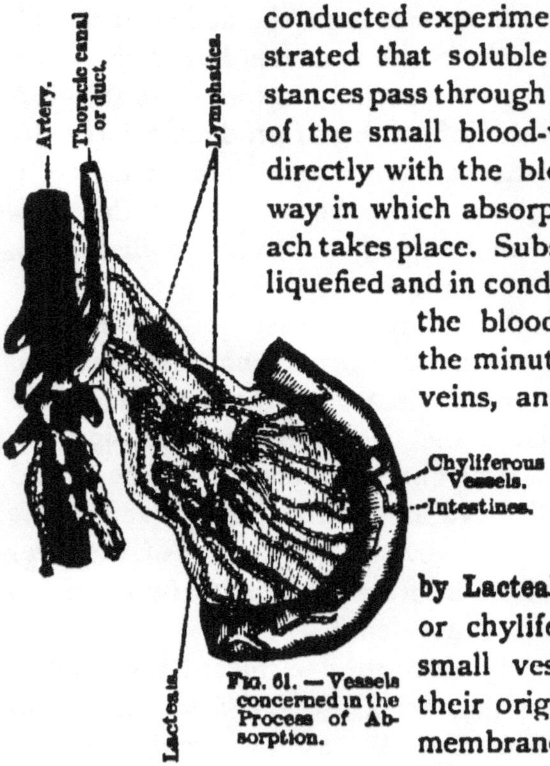

129. Absorption by Lacteals.—The lacteals or chyliferous vessels are small vessels which have their origin in the mucous membrane lining the small intestine.   It is through them that the greater part of the digested food is absorbed from the small intestine and transferred to the circulatory system. This absorption is carried on as follows: projecting from the lining membrane of the small intestine are vast numbers of delicate, hair-like projections, about

FIG. 61. — Vessels concerned in the Process of Absorption.

Artery.

Thoracic canal or duct.

Lymphatics.

Chyliferous Vessels.

Intestines.

Lacteals.

one-third of an inch in length, which are called *villi*. In each of these villi are numerous small blood-vessels and lacteals. The villi dip into the digested and liquefied food substance, which is thus taken up into the lacteals, and by them finally transferred into the circulatory system. The blood-vessels in the villi also directly absorb a portion of the food, just as is done in the stomach. The liquefied food which is found in the lacteals during the period of digestion is a milky white fluid and is called *chyle*.

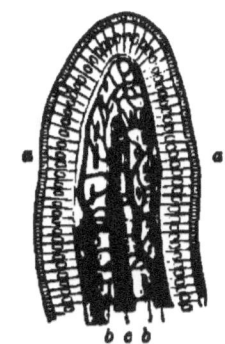

130. The Lymphatics.—The lymphatics are very small vessels which exist beneath the skin and in all the mucous membranes of the body. These vessels are similar in appearance to the lacteals, and they carry a transparent, colorless liquid called *lymph*. They exist in large numbers, and as they proceed in their course they pass through certain glands called *lymphatic glands*, where numerous corpuscles resembling the white corpuscles of the blood are formed. These corpuscles are carried away from the glands by the stream of lymph which flows through them. Finally, the lymphatics unite with some of the lacteals at the back of the abdomen and form a vessel called the thoracic duct. This thoracic duct, passing up the body in front of the spinal column, opens directly into one of the large veins of the body, and the nourishing fluid which is carried by the lacteals, together with the lymph and lymph corpuscles, is thus mixed with the venous blood, and emptied immediately into the right auricle of the heart.

FIG 62.—SECTION OF A VILLUS (highly magnified).

a, a.—Covering of Villus.

b, b.—Capillaries.

c.—Lacteal.

REVIEW—FOOD AND DIGESTION.

Food is necessary in order to supply materials for the repair of the worn-out tissues of the body.

The process by which the food is prepared to be taken into the blood is called digestion.

The process by which the digested food is taken from the digestive organs and transferred to the circulatory system is called absorption.

The process by which the elements of nutrition are taken from the blood and become changed into living tissues is called assimilation.

Food principles are of three classes: inorganic, organic nitrogenized, and organic non-nitrogenized.

The most important inorganic food principles are water, salt, phosphate of lime; the organic nitrogenized principles are meats, albumen, casein, gluten, etc.; the organic non-nitrogenized principles are sugars, fats, and starches.

Water is the only substance that will quench thirst. Milk, tea, coffee, chocolate, and other substances are healthful drinks, but it is only the water which they contain that quenches thirst.

The organs of mastication are the teeth, the tongue, the lips, and the cheeks. The saliva assists in mastication and also in digestion.

The teeth may be preserved from decay if properly cared for.

In the process of swallowing, the food passes from the mouth into the pharynx, from the pharynx into the esophagus, and thence into the stomach.

The nitrogenized foods are digested in the stomach, by the action of the gastric juice.

The fats, starches, and sugars are digested in the small intestine. Three fluids assist in this intestinal digestion. The liver and the pancreas are important organs and secrete fluids which aid in digestion.

Absorption takes place from the stomach and from the small intestine. Fluids and nitrogenized food principles are absorbed directly by the blood-vessels. The emulsified fats and other substances are absorbed by the lacteals.

The principal alcoholic drinks are beer, cider, wine, whisky, brandy, rum, etc.

Alcoholic drinks are produced by fermentation or distillation. They do not quench thirst, but create an unnatural thirst.

Beer of whatever kind contains alcohol. Alcohol, taken even in very small quantities, has the peculiar power of exciting a desire for more. The drinking of beer or cider is almost certain to awaken an appetite for stronger drinks. The only safe rule is to abstain entirely from the use of anything that contains alcohol.

Whiskies, brandies, and wines are seldom pure. They are adulterated with various substances in order to impart to them a desired flavor, taste, or color.

Alcohol interferes with digestion. It causes diseases of the stomach, heartburn, nausea, vomiting, incurable dyspepsia. It causes fatty degeneration of the liver, hob-nailed liver, and interferes with the secretion of the bile. It hinders the proper nutrition of the system, and prepares the way for disease.

Tobacco is of no possible value, either as a food or as a drink. It interferes with the mastication of the food. It hinders digestion.

CHAPTER XV.

THE SKIN.

131. The Skin.—The skin is a tough, elastic structure which covers the entire surface of the body. It is estimated that the skin surface in an adult is equal to about sixteen square feet. The skin varies in thickness in different parts of its surface. Where it is exposed to friction and pressure it is quite thick, as on the soles of the feet and palms of the hands. At the edges of the openings into the body it merges into, and is continuous with, the mucous membrane.

132. Uses of the Skin.—The skin is one of the most important structures of the body, and it performs many functions, among which are the following :—

(1) It forms a protective covering for the surface of the body;

(2) It aids in equalizing the temperature of the body;

(3) It acts as an organ of excretion, removing certain waste matters from the body.

133. Structure of the Skin.—The skin consists of two layers—an inner one, called the *true skin*, or *derma*, and an outer one, called the *cuticle*, or *epidermis*, or scarfskin.

The true skin merges with the fatty tissues beneath it. In this layer of the skin is found blood-vessels, nerves, and glands.

The cuticle, or epidermis, which is the outer layer of

the skin, contains neither blood-vessels nor nerves. It is composed entirely of cells, and contains a peculiar matter called pigment-ary matter, which gives to the skin its color or complexion. This mat-ter varies in color; in the negro it is almost black. The outer cells of the cuticle are flat, hard, and horny-like. The cuticle serves as a protection to the delicate structures of the true skin, and varies in thickness as the parts are more or less exposed to friction.

Fig. 63.—Section of Skin (magnified).
1.—Epidermis. 4.—Coloring matter.
2.—Derma or true skin. 5.—Nerve termination
3.—Hair follicle. 6.—Sweat gland.

134. The Hair and the Nails.—These are both appendages of the skin. Hairs exist on nearly the whole surface of the body, and vary in size and length. The roots of the hairs are imbedded in small openings in the skin, called hair follicles. These follicles are from $\frac{1}{17}$ to $\frac{1}{4}$ of an inch in depth. The shaft of the hair is that part outside the skin; it consists of hard, flat cells, covering a fibrous center. This center contains pig-mentary matter, upon which the color of the hair de-pends. Hair is not supplied with blood-vessels, but obtains its nourishment by absorption from the true skin.

The nails begin near the tips of the fingers and the
toes; they consist of two parts, a root and a body. The
body of the nail is that part which is exposed to sight; the
root is about one-fourth the length of the body, and is
closely adherent to the true skin underneath. The nails
are really modifications of the cuticle, or scarfskin,
and have the same general structure.

135. Uses of the Hair and the Nails.—The hairs have
several important uses. They serve to protect certain parts and organs of the body. The
hair on the head and face protects these
parts from cold, and in extremely hot
weather shields them from the burning
rays of the sun. The eyebrows prevent
perspiration from running down upon the
eyelids, and the eyelashes protect the eye
from the entrance of dust and other foreign substances.

FIG. 64.—ORIGIN
OF A HAIR (very
highly magni-
fied).
A.—The follicle.
B.—The root.

The nails serve as protection to the
ends of the fingers and toes, and aid the fingers in taking hold of, and picking up small articles.

136. Perspiration.—It has already been explained how
carbonic acid and other poisonous matters produced by
the decomposition of tissues are removed from the system through the lungs. The skin also serves to elimi-
nate certain waste materials from the body; this process of elimination is produced by the perspiration, or
sweat. This function of the skin is very important. If the
skin were to be covered with an impervious coating, such
as varnish, so as to prevent perspiration or sweating,
death would soon ensue. The quantity of perspiration
varies according to the conditions of the weather, the

amount of exercise taken, and the character and quantity of food and drink introduced into the body. The average amount of sweat secreted by the skin is about two pints daily. There is constantly more or less sweat being secreted, and it is the evaporation of this which does so much toward equalizing the heat of the body.

137. Glands of the Skin.—There are two kinds of glands found in the skin. One of these is called *sebaceous glands*, the other *sudoriparous* or sweat-glands.

The sebaceous glands are small glands which open by a duct into the hair follicles. They secrete an oily substance which serves to keep the hair and skin soft and pliable. The sweat-glands are the most numerous and most important, and every portion of the skin is supplied with them. They consist merely of a small tube, opening on the outside of the skin and coiled

FIG. 65.—SURFACE OF THE SKIN.

1, 1, 1, 1.—Openings of the sweat-glands.
2, 2, 2, 2.—Grooves between the papillæ.

up just below the true skin. These are the glands which secrete perspiration.

138. Other Uses of the Skin.—Besides serving as a protection to the surface of the body, helping to equalize the temperature, and assisting in the elimination of useless waste matters, the skin has other important functions. It serves as an organ of sensation, for in it are situated the nerves which convey the sense of touch, pain, and temperature. It assists in the respiratory process, for it absorbs oxygen to a slight extent and exhales carbonic acid gas. It has also an absorptive power by which certain substances may be transferred from its outer surface into the capillaries and veins, and thus into the system.

139. Effects of Alcohol on the Skin.—If you should place pure alcohol upon the skin, and then cover it with a piece of rubber, so that it cannot evaporate, the alcohol would act in the same manner as a mustard plaster—irritating the skin and perhaps blistering it. When taken into the body, alcohol circulates with the blood and has similar bad effects upon the skin, congesting it and predisposing it to various forms of skin eruptions, causing much discomfort and itching and burning of the skin. This effect of alcohol upon the skin is frequently seen in persons who are hard drinkers, their faces being reddened and blotched and otherwise disfigured.

140. Injuries and Diseases of the Skin.—Probably the most common injury to the skin is that caused by burning or scalding. If the skin be burned throughout its entire thickness, a scar always results. The pain accompanying a burn is very severe; it may be relieved by protecting the injured part from the air. Moistened baking soda, sweet oil, and linseed oil are valuable for this purpose. If none of these are at hand, flour slightly moistened will answer the purpose. The burned surface should be covered completely with one of these substances. Eruptions of the skin are often caused by indigestion. The skin is frequently injured and permanently disfigured by the use of cosmetics designed to improve the complexion. Corns are a thickening of the scarfskin, and are usually caused by the wearing of ill-fitting shoes.

CHAPTER XVI.

CARE OF THE SKIN—CLOTHING.

141. Cleanliness of the Skin.—In order that the skin may be in a condition to perform its several important functions, it is very necessary that it should be kept clean. The perspiration contains much waste matter, which, by its evaporation, soon accumulates upon the surface of the skin. The sebaceous glands constantly secrete an oily matter, which also tends to accumulate. The outer layer of the skin, the cuticle, is constantly wearing out, forming bran-like scales, which, together with dust and dirt, are caught in the drying perspiration, and remain on the surface of the skin. All these things, by their accumulation, fill and choke up the openings of the glands, interfering with the discharge of their secretions, and with the comfort and health of the body.

To maintain a proper and healthy condition of the skin and consequently of the entire system, all these accumulations of waste matter and dirt should be removed, and, so far as possible, prevented. The only way in which this can properly be done is by bathing.

142. Bathing.—Baths are of great importance to the general system, keeping the skin clean and healthy, quickening the circulation, and adding to one's personal enjoyment and bodily vigor. Bathing should be indulged in often. A bath should be taken every day, if convenient; if not convenient daily, then take a bath at least once a week, thoroughly washing the whole body.

The cold bath is the most stimulating and strengthening, and if followed by a good rubbing with a coarse towel, will rarely produce any chilly or uncomfortable sensations. The cold bath causes the skin to become rosy, the heart to beat more vigorously, and the whole system to feel a sense of comfort and well-being. The warm bath, though very useful in removing the dirt from the skin, and though feeling more pleasant to the bather, is nearly always followed by a sense of languor and exhaustion. The skin is left in a relaxed condition, which makes it very easy for the person to contract colds. After taking a warm bath quite a time should elapse before going into the open air.

Do not take a bath soon after a meal, and while digestion is going on. Wait until two or three hours after you have eaten. When bathing, do not stay in the water too long. Three to five minutes is long enough for a cold bath, and ten to fifteen minutes for a warm one.

Strong soap should never be used on the skin. Such soap contains much alkali, and this tends to remove the oily matter from the skin, rendering it harsh and rough. It removes more of the cuticle than is advisable. In bathing use only as much soap as is necessary for cleanliness, thereby keeping the skin smooth, soft, and pliable.

The hair and scalp should be kept clean, the same as the rest of the body. Give the scalp a thorough washing and rubbing at least once a week. It is very important also that the teeth and nails should be kept clean.

143. Clothing.—One of the main objects of clothing is to keep the body at a comfortable temperature. The clothing should consequently vary in kind and quantity, according to the climate, and according to the needs of the body. In cold weather it is well to wear, next to the skin, clothing made of such material as will not readily conduct the heat from the body. Woolen goods, flannels, and furs, are materials of this class. In hot weather, linen, cotton, and silk are worn, as these materials conduct the heat from the body, thus reducing its temperature and producing comfort. Light colors are cooler than dark ones in the summer time.

Clothing should vary in amount according to the condition of the weather. The outside clothing should be such as can be changed to meet the different requirements. Over-clothes of different weights should be used according as the weather is cold or warm.

The feet should always be well covered, and care should be taken to keep them dry. The neck and face should not be bundled up closely, even in very cold weather, for, by so doing, colds and soreness of the throat are more likely to be contracted.

144. Effects of Alcohol on the Skin.—Alcohol is responsible for many diseases of the skin. A clear skin and a healthy complexion are unknown in persons addicted to the alcohol habit; they may have what we call a florid complexion, but it is neither natural nor healthy. Persons who would have natural, healthy complexions should let alcohol in all its forms absolutely alone. The same may be said with reference to the inveterate use of tobacco, which frequently produces a tawny color in the skin.

CHAPTER XVII.

THE NERVOUS SYSTEM.

145. What is the Nervous System?—The nervous system, although in a certain sense distinct from all the other systems, unites the various parts and organs into one complete organic whole. It is the medium through which all impressions upon the mind are received and appreciated. It regulates the movements of the body and all the processes of life. It comprises:—

(1) The *cerebro-spinal* system;

(2) The *sympathetic* system.

146. Nervous Tissue.—Nervous tissue is either white or gray in color, and consists of two structures, *nerve-cells* and *nerve-fibers*. The nerve-cells are the parts that are capable of creating nerve force.

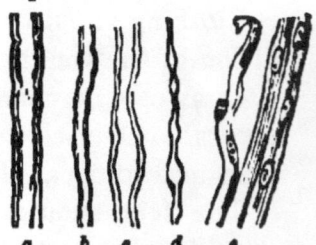

Fig. 66.—Nerve-Fibers. (Highly magnified.)

The nerve-fibers do not create nerve force, but act as conductors of this force after it has been generated by the nerve-cells. The nerve-cells form the gray matter and the nerve-fibers the white matter of nervous tissue. Every nerve-fiber is connected with a nerve-cell.

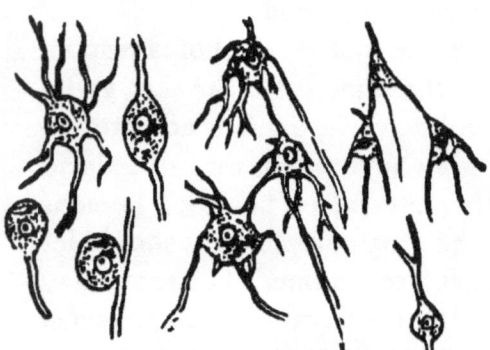

Fig. 67.—Nerve-Cells. (Highly magnified.)

147. The Nerves.—A group or collection of nerve-cells forms a nerve center; from each nerve center pass great numbers of nerve-fibers, arranged in bundles, into different parts of the body, the bundles dividing and sub-dividing as they proceed. The bundles of nerve-fibers form white, glistening cords, called nerves. These nerves penetrate every part of the body.

148. Motor and Sensory Nerves. —Nerves contain two kinds of nerve-fibers; one of these conducts *to* the nerve centers, the other conducts *from* the nerve centers to the muscles or organs. Nerves of the first kind are called sensory nerves; the others are called motor nerves.

Fig. 68.—A Nerve and its Branches.

We may illustrate the action of these two kinds of nerves as follows: If one should place a finger on a hot stove, the sensation of pain would travel to the nerve center through the sensory nerves; in the nerve center there is then generated a peculiar force, which, being conducted from it to the muscle through the motor nerves, causes the muscle to contract and thus to remove the finger from its uncomfortable position.

149. Nerve Current.—This passing of sensation to a nerve center and of force back to the muscle from the nerve center constitutes what is called the nerve current. It is estimated that the rapidity of this current is

about 110 feet in a second, much slower than an electric
current.   It requires one-twentieth of a second for a

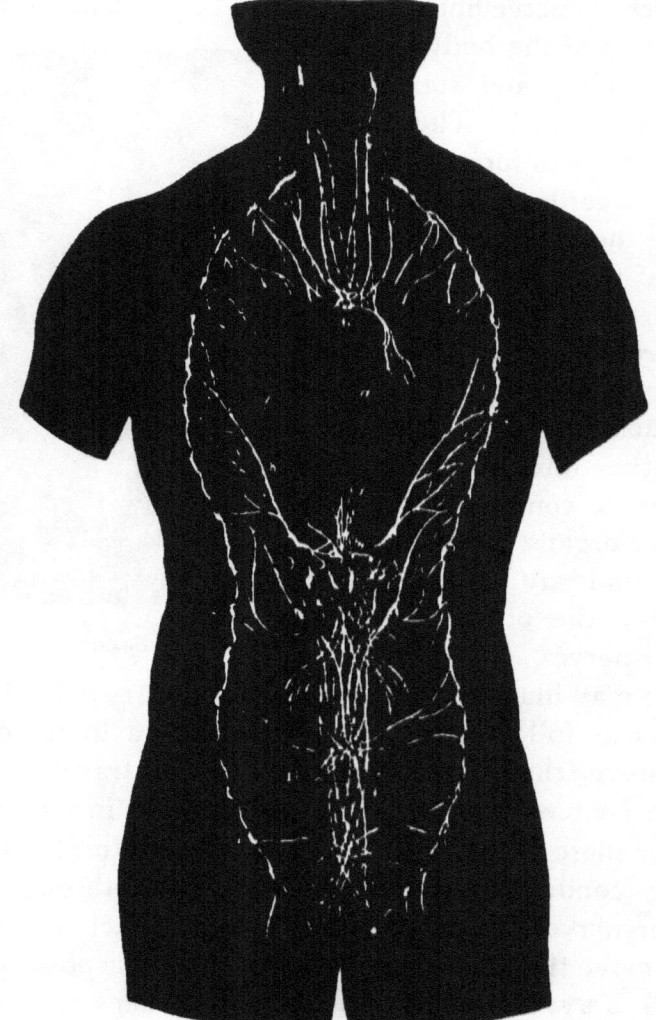

Fig. 69.—The Sympathetic Nerve System.

sensation to travel from the foot to the brain, and an
equal time for the force generated to travel back.

150. Varieties of Motor and Sensory Nerves.—By the nerves we are enabled to appreciate many different sensations. We accordingly have many nerves of sensation. Hearing, seeing, feeling, tasting, and smelling are all different kinds of sensation, and there are special nerve centers which preside over each. Of the motor nerves also there are several varieties, some coming from centers which preside over muscles, others from those which preside over the heart and stomach, and so on.

Certain motor nerves, called the *vaso-motor* nerves, are distributed to the walls of the blood-vessels, and control the circulation by regulating the size of the blood-vessels, causing them to dilate or to contract in proportion to the amount of blood that is required.

151. The Sympathetic System.—The sympathetic system consists of nerves and nerve centers. The nerves are composed of nerve-fibers · and the nerve centers, or *ganglions*, as they are called, are composed of nerve-cells. There are two chains of ganglions, one on each side of the spinal column, within the body, running its whole length (see Fig. 69). There are thirty pairs of these ganglions. The sympathetic system of nerves supplies the involuntary muscular tissue, governs all acts of secretion, equalizes the circulation, and governs the nutrition of the body. The nerves from the ganglions are distributed to the mucous membranes and to the organs concerned in nutrition, namely the stomach, liver, intestines, etc. The vaso-motor nerves belong to this system of nerves.

152. The Cerebro-Spinal System.—This system of nerves consists of the brain and spinal cord, and the nerves which come from them. This is the system of nerves that supplies the greater part of the body. It

o

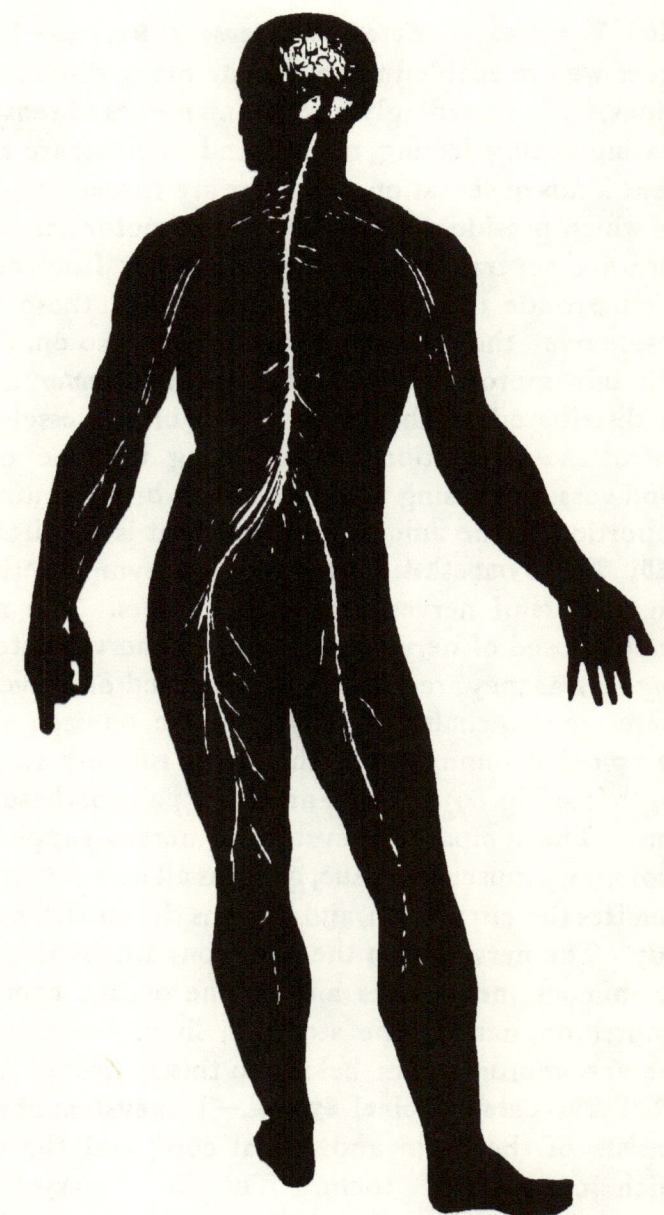

FIG. 70.—THE CEREBRO-SPINAL SYSTEM.

presides over sensation, the special senses, voluntary
motion, intellect, and all the movements which charac-
terize different individuals.

153. The Brain.—The brain is a mass of nervous tissue contained within the cranium.   It is composed of a
number of ganglions,
or nerve centers,
which are connected
with one another and
with the motor and
the sensory nerves of
the system.   It con-
sists of both white
and gray matter. Its
average weight is
about three pounds
in men, and four or

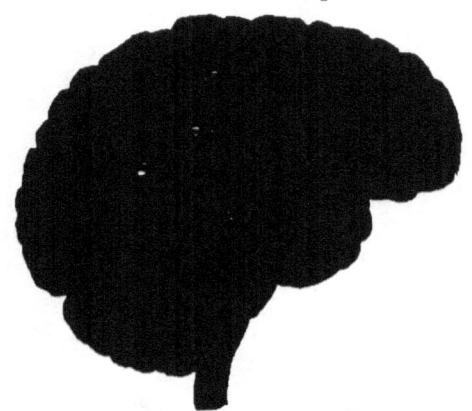

FIG. 71.—SIDE VIEW OF THE BRAIN.

five ounces less than this in women.   The brain consists of three portions, called the *cerebrum*, the *cerebellum*, and the *medulla oblongata*.

154. The Cerebrum.—The cerebrum comprises the
greater portion of the brain, forming almost its entire
mass. It is divided into two halves, called hemispheres,
by a deep fissure, running from the front backward. It
is composed of both white and gray matter—the white
matter forming the interior, while the gray matter lies
on the surface.   The surface of the cerebrum is not
smooth, but is arranged in large wrinkles called convolutions.   This arrangement on the surface gives room for
more gray matter than would be possible if the surface
were smooth.   The whole mass of the cerebrum is covered with membrane, and is contained within the cranium.

155. Functions of the Cerebrum.—The cerebrum is the organ of intelligence. It is in man that it reaches its highest development. Usually, but not always, the degree of intelligence varies with the size of the brain.

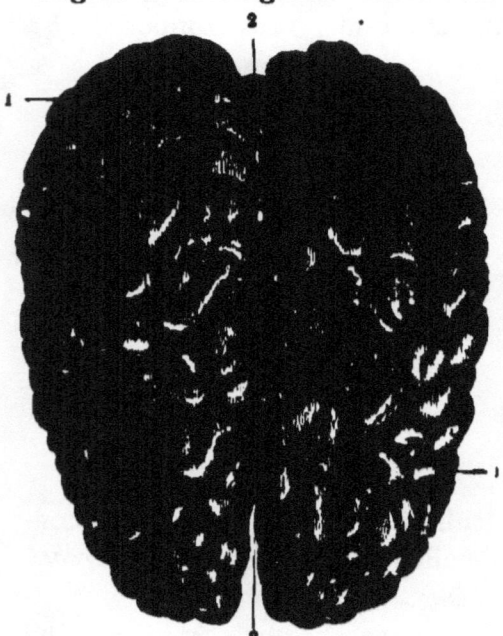

In animals the brain, when compared with that of man, is very small in proportion to the size of the body. The brain of an idiot is usually small and imperfectly developed.

All operations of thought and intellect take place in the cerebrum. If this part of the brain be removed from a bird or other small animal, it immediately becomes stupid and utterly indifferent to

Fig. 72.—View of the Top of the Brain.
1.1.—Convolutions.
2.2.—Division between the hemispheres.

its surroundings. It still possesses power of motion and sensation, and can still see and hear, but it connects no idea with anything heard or seen, and is totally indifferent to everything. It may feel hungry or thirsty, but it has no idea of relieving its hunger or thirst by eating or drinking.

156. Injuries and Diseases of the Cerebrum.—Different portions of the cerebrum perform different functions.. If it be injured or become diseased, then the function of a portion of it may be changed or destroyed. Thus there may be diseased conditions which cause paralysis of particular muscles or of one whole side of the body. Certain diseases of the cerebrum may cause a person to be deprived of the power of speaking, or of writing, or of both. In all diseased conditions of the cerebrum, the mind is affected in one way or another.

157. The Cerebellum.—This portion of the brain weighs about five ounces. It is situated beneath the back

Cerebrum.

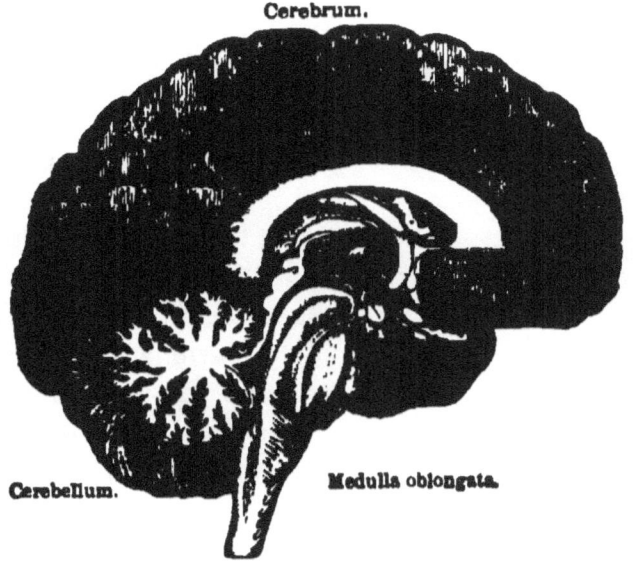

Cerebellum.   Medulla oblongata.

FIG. 73.—SECTIONAL VIEW OF THE BRAIN.

part of the cerebrum, and is connected with it. It is composed of white matter within and gray matter without. Its surface is rough, being arranged in thin layers, or folds. It consists of two halves or hemispheres, and is much more fully developed in man than in any other animal.

158. Functions of the Cerebellum.—There are differences of opinion as to the exact functions of this part of the brain, and we may say that all of its functions have not as yet been satisfactorily ascertained. Its principal business, however, is undoubtedly to preside over co-ordinate muscular movements, especially those used in walking (see Definitions, p. 182). If this part of the brain be injured or diseased, the power of locomotion is greatly hindered, the muscles not acting together as they should.

159. The Medulla Oblongata.—This portion of the brain connects the spinal cord with the various ganglions of the brain. It is about an inch and a quarter in length and an inch wide. It is composed of a mass of white matter, within which is imbedded a collection of gray matter or nerve-cells. The medulla oblongata, by connecting the spinal cord with the brain, serves to conduct the sensation and motor stimulus to and from the brain. Its most import-

FIG. 74.—THE BRAIN AND SPINAL CORD.

ant function however, is in connection with respiration. The small mass of gray matter within the medulla ob-longata has entire control over the acts of respiration, and if it be injured or destroyed, breathing ceases and death is the result. This mass of gray matter has aptly been called the " vital point."

160. The Spinal Cord.—The spinal cord is that part of the nervous system which extends through the spinal canal from the brain to almost the lower end of the spinal column. It is composed of gray matter internally and white matter externally. From it are given off thirty-one pairs of nerves which, leaving it at different points, divide and sub-divide and go to all parts of the trunk and limbs.

161. Functions of the Spinal Cord and Spinal Nerves.—The spinal nerves rise from the spinal cord by two roots. The one in front is called the anterior root, the other the pos-terior root. Both sensation and motion are conducted by these nerves; the sensation is conveyed from the parts to the spinal cord

FIG. 75.—SECTION OF SPINAL CORD.
(Showing Roots of Spinal Nerves.)

through the posterior roots, and the motor power is conveyed from the spinal cord to the parts through the anterior roots. On the posterior root of each nerve tnere is a small ganglion, or knot of nervous matter. If the anterior root of a spinal nerve be cut or divided, sensation in that nerve is not affected, but the motor power is lost; if the posterior root be divided, the power of motion is not impaired, but sensation is lost

This shows that the anterior root contains motor nerves; the posterior root, sensory ones. The spinal cord acts as a conductor between the nerves and the brain. It also acts as a nerve center, generating nerve force. This force is generated independently of the brain and produces certain actions known as reflex actions. A frog may be beheaded, and if its foot be pricked with a pin, it will draw its foot up out of danger. This is a reflex act and the force generating it is independent of the brain and thought.

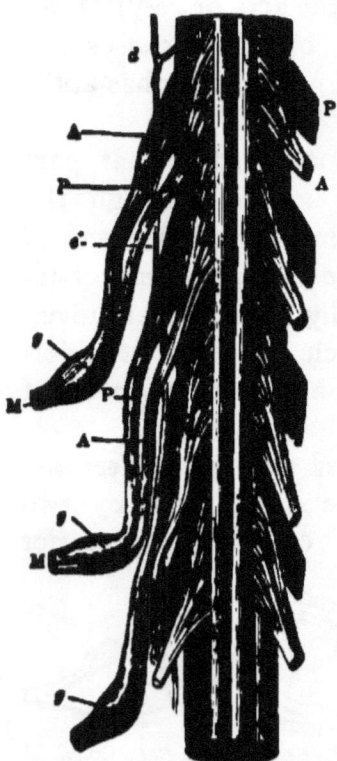

Fig. 76.—How the Spinal Nerves are Given Off from the Spinal Cord.

A, A, A.—Anterior roots.
P, P, P.—Posterior roots.
c, d.—Filaments passing between the posterior roots.
g, g, g.—Ganglions of posterior roots.
M, M.—Nerves formed by union of two roots.
(The size of the roots is not so large in nature as here represented.)

162. Diseases of the Spinal Cord.—Diseases and injuries of the spinal cord always affect motion and sensation below the diseased portion. Sometimes injury or disease so affects the cord as to destroy its communication with the brain. In such cases there is paralysis of the lower part of the body, and although voluntary motion is no longer possible, reflex action still exists.

163. Effects of Alcohol on the Brain.—Alcohol is a deadly enemy to the brain and spinal cord. When it is taken into the body its effects are felt by the entire nervous system. It acts directly upon the nervous tissues. The vaso-motor nerves are paralyzed, allowing the small blood-vessels to dilate, thus producing a flushed appearance of the skin. The heart's action is quickened on account of the paralyzing effect of the alcohol on the nerves governing its action. Alcohol causes a sense of exhilaration and well-being for a short time after it is taken, but when the alcohol effect has worn off, the whole system is left in an exhausted state. To renew this feeling of exhilaration alcoholic drinks are often resorted to, resulting after awhile in the formation of the most dangerous and injurious of all habits, that of alcohol drinking.

Intoxication.—When alcohol is taken into the body its immediate effects vary with the quantity that has been taken. With considerable quantities there is first a stage of excitement and exhilaration, the person easily giving way to his emotions. He laughs or cries, is happy or morose. Then he begins to lose control of his muscles; his under lip falls and his tongue becomes paralyzed to such an extent that he is unable to talk plainly. His intellect becomes so muddled that he cannot talk or act with any intelligence, and his whole moral nature seems to be changed. At the same time his muscles refuse to act in their natural way; they become weak and tremulous, and he goes staggering along, scarcely able to stand. If an extremely large quantity of alcohol has been taken he soon becomes insensible, lying as though dead, with all the muscles relaxed. This is the usual course of intoxication.

After the person recovers from his intoxication, he suffers with general depression, headache, dizziness, and great nervousness for quite a while; showing that the system has been under the influence of a most powerful poison.

Alcohol users are generally troubled with sleeplessness, and what little sleep they are able to obtain is disturbed by distressing dreams.

Delirium Tremens.—This is one of the most frightful nervous diseases known. It is always caused by the continued and excessive use of alcohol. A person addicted to the use of alcohol sometimes goes on a prolonged debauch, drinking day and night, and scarcely eating any food. Pretty soon the whole nervous system is exhausted and the mind becomes deranged. He cannot sleep and everything around appears to him to be some living object. His face becomes haggard, his eyes bloodshot, and his gait unsteady. He is in mortal terror of everything, and in his disordered mind he imagines that he sees insects, snakes, devils, and other horrible objects around him, mocking him and ready to pounce upon him and do him injury. He cannot eat and cannot sleep, and if relief is not soon afforded him, death occurs. If he recovers, he is a mental and physical wreck for a long time afterwards.

Chronic Alcoholism.—A person who persists in the use of alcoholic drinks sooner or later becomes a chronic alcohol drinker. Our poorhouses and penitentiaries are filled with just this class of men. A man may be of good moral character, ambitious and successful, but when he becomes a confirmed drinker all this is changed. He becomes immoral, he loses his self-respect, and his ambition; he cares no longer for success in life, and sooner or later he goes to the poorhouse, the penitentiary, or the drunkard's grave. Many men who were once good men, have been brought to poverty and degradation by this giant evil, alcohol drinking. Chronic drinkers are often subject to serious nervous diseases. Alcohol acts directly upon the nervous tissue causing it to become diseased. Paralysis of different organs and parts of the body often occurs. Neuralgias are of common occurrence, and sometimes the mind itself becomes affected.

164. Effects of Tobacco on the Nervous System.—A very frequent cause of nervousness is undoubtedly the use of tobacco. The poisonous element called nicotine, which is contained in all tobacco, when absorbed into the system, affects the whole nervous organism. For this reason, persons engaged in work which requires great care and accuracy, necessarily abstain from the use of tobacco. For this reason, tobacco is especially injurious to the young, making them weak mentally as well as physically.

It is the influence of this poison on the nerves of the heart which frequently changes its action and produces in many persons a diseased condition called the "tobacco heart."

By causing a constant nervous irritability, tobacco, as we have already noticed, retards the nutrition. Often the inveterate tobacco user becomes pale, nervous, and thin, but when he gives up his tobacco he again becomes hale and hearty.

Cigarette Smoking.—"Scarcely less injurious, in a subtle and generally unrecognized way, than the habit of taking 'nips' of alcohol between meals, is the growing practice of smoking cigarettes incessantly," says a writer in that famous medical journal, the *London Lancet.* "It

is against the habit of smoking cigarettes in large quantities, with the belief that these miniature doses of nicotine are innocuous, we desire to enter a protest. The
truth is that, perhaps owing to the way the tobacco leaf
is shredded, coupled with the fact that it is brought into
more direct relation with the mouth and air passages
than when it is smoked in a pipe or cigar, the effects
produced on the nervous system by a free consumption
of cigarettes are more marked and characteristic than
those recognizable after recourse to other modes of
smoking. A pulse-tracing, made after the subject has
smoked a dozen cigarettes, will, as a rule, be flatter and
more indicative of depression than one taken after the
smoking of cigars. It is no uncommon practice for
young men who smoke cigarettes habitually to consume
from eight to twelve in an hour, and to keep this up
for four or five hours daily. The total quantity of tobacco used may not seem large, but, beyond question,
the volume of smoke to which the breath organs of the
smoker are exposed, and the characteristics of that smoke
as regards the proportion of nicotine introduced into
the system, combine to place the organism very fully
under the influence of the tobacco. A considerable
number of cases have been brought under our notice
during the last few months, in which youths and young
men who have not yet completed the full term of physical development have had their health seriously impaired by the practice of almost incessantly smoking
cigarettes. It is well that the facts should be known,
as the impression evidently prevails that any number of
these little 'whiffs' must needs be perfectly innocuous,
whereas they often do infinite harm."

165. Effects of Opium upon the Nervous System.—Opium is a narcotic poison which is obtained from the juice of the poppy. It has, perhaps, the most decided effect of all drugs upon the nervous system. It should never be taken in any form into the body, except by the direction of a reliable physician. It acts on the whole nervous system, relieving all forms of pain and giving to the person ease and comfort. It is this effect of opium which lures so many into the habit of taking it. It is an exceedingly fascinating drug, producing a happy, comfortable feeling of the mind. The habit of using it is easy to acquire, but is by far the most difficult to overcome.

An opium eater or smoker is to be pitied, for as the habit grows on him his mental and moral faculties are ruined. He loses all honor and self-respect. He will lie, steal, or commit any crime to gratify his habit. He soon becomes a complete wreck; he cannot cure himself of the habit, for as soon as his opium is given up he suffers the most acute mental and physical anguish, and is forced to its use again in order to obtain relief. Thus he exists until death comes to his relief, taking him off many years earlier than it would had he not acquired this deplorable habit.

The most common preparations of opium are morphine, laudanum and paregoric. Many patent medicines, especially soothing syrups for babies, contain opium in some form. All these should be avoided, for they are all more or less dangerous.

166. Other Narcotics.—Chloral and cocaine are two drugs which are most injurious in their effects upon the nervous system if used to excess. Chloral acts by numbing the nerve centers, thus producing deep sleep —not a natural but an artificial sleep. If this drug be used habitually, the nervous system is soon wrecked and the physical energies exhausted. Cocaine produces much the same effects as opium. It is the most fascinating drug known, and the habit of using it is the most injurious and fatal to life. The nerves are shattered, the physical health is ruined, the intellect is weakened, and death comes early as the result of its continued use.

Tea and coffee, although mild in their action, are classified among narcotics. They both have a decided influence upon the nervous system, and if they are used to excess their effects are very likely to be injurious to the whole system. Especially are the injurious effects of these drinks noticeable in young and growing persons, and in persons of a highly nervous temperament. Children who indulge in tea and coffee become nervous and often irritable, and their nervous system is apparently under a sort of stimulation which renders its proper and healthy development impossible. The best drinks for one having a healthy, strong body, are water and milk, and, generally speaking, the less tea and coffee taken the better it is for one's nervous system. The drinking of tea and coffee, with many people, sometimes produces headache and dizziness, and generally a tired and languid feeling, but sometimes the opposite effect, restlessness and sleeplessness. On the other hand, it is a well proved fact that tea and coffee are often helpful to persons who labor hard either with hand or brain. There are indeed times when they seem to be useful in helping to quiet the nerves and rest the tired brain. These beneficial effects are experienced generally by adults and elderly people.

CHAPTER XVIII.

SEEING.

167. The Special Senses.—The senses which enable us to appreciate the properties of external objects are called *special senses.* They are: seeing, hearing, smelling, tasting, and feeling or touch.

168. The Eye.—The eye is the organ of seeing. The eyeball is a ball-shaped body, about one inch in diameter. The wall or shell of the eyeball is composed of three layers, or membranes. The outer one of these layers is the toughest and hardest, and is called the *sclerotic coat.* It forms what is usually known as the white of the eye. It surrounds the whole eyeball except a small portion in front, which is covered with a transparent membrane called the *cornea.*

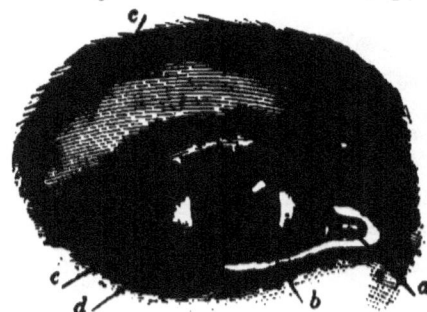

FIG. 77.—THE EYE.

a.—Nasal duct for passage of tears into the nose.
b.—Iris.
c.—Position of tear gland.
d.—Pupil.
e.—Sclerotic coat of the eye.

The middle layer, or membrane, lies just within the sclerotic coat; it contains numerous blood-vessels, and is of a dark color. This layer is called the *choroid coat* of the eyeball. Within this is the third layer, or mem-

brane, called the *retina*. This is a very delicate structure containing a complicated arrangement of nervous
tissue. The sensation of sight is received from the
retina.

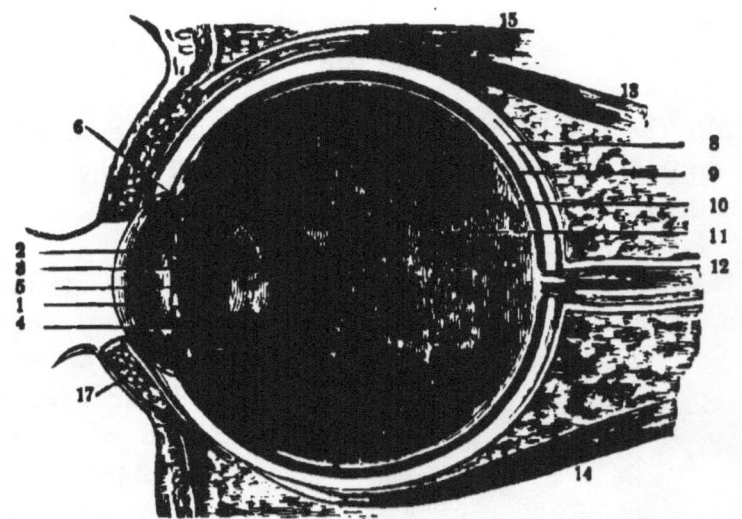

Fig. 78.—Vertical Section of the Eyeball.

1.—Cornea.	6.—Ciliary processes.	11.—Vitreous humor.
2.—Aqueous humor.	7.—Canal around the lens.	12.—Optic nerve.
3.—Pupil.	8.—Sclerotic coat.	13, 14, 15.—Muscles of the
4.—Iris.	9.—Choroid coat.	eyeball and eyelid.
5.—Crystalline lens.	10.—Retina.	

The interior of the eyeball is filled with a clear, transparent, jelly-like substance, called the *vitreous humor*.
Just in front of the vitreous humor and behind the
cornea is a small transparent body, called the *crystalline lens*, and in front of this lens is a sort of curtain
with a circular opening in its center. This curtain
is called the *iris*, and the opening in it forms the *pupil*
of the eye. Between the crystalline lens and the cornea
is a small space filled with a clear fluid called the *aqueous humor*.

169. Movements of the Eyeball.—The eyeball is capable of being turned about in all directions. Fastened to the sclerotic coat are six small muscles, which produce these movements by their contractions.

FIG. 79.—SECTION OF THE EYE.

1, 2, 3, 4, 5.—Muscles of the eyeball.
6.—Lacrymal gland, with its ducts, 7, 8, 9.

Sometimes certain of these muscles lose their power of contraction or become weak. When this happens it causes cross-eyes or strabismus.

170. The Optic Nerve.—The optic nerve, or nerve of sight, enters each eyeball from behind, and divides into many small branches in the retina. The fibers of the optic nerves mingle in such a way that often an injury to one eye also affects the sight of the other.

171. The Eyelids.—The eyelids are folds of skin lined with a delicate mucous membrane, which may be drawn over the front of the eyeball. In each eyelid are numerous small glands, that secrete an oily substance. This substance, covering the edge of the lids, prevents the overflow of tears upon the cheek. The eyelids protect the front of the eyeball from the entrance of foreign bodies. They also protect the eye from too strong light.

10

172. The Tear Gland.—At the outer side of the eyeball and within the socket is a small gland, the *lacrymal gland*, whose object it is to secrete tears. The tears secreted flow through a duct and then are spread out upon the eyeball.

A certain amount of this secretion is being constantly formed. It serves to keep the eyeball moist, and prevents friction between it and the eyelids; if dust or any foreign substance enters the

TEAR GLAND

FIG. 80.—POSITION OF THE TEAR GLAND.

eye, the tears are poured out in abundance, and help to wash this matter from the eye.

At the inner angle of the eyelids is a small opening. This is the opening of the nasal duct, a duct extending from the eye into the nose. Through this duct the tears are constantly drained from the eye; if, however, they are too abundant to pass through the duct, they overflow, and run down upon the cheeks.

173. How we See.—If a double convex lens is held a certain distance from a screen of ground glass, an image of the objects in front of the lens is formed upon the screen (see Definitions, page 186). This image is small, and certain objects which are near or

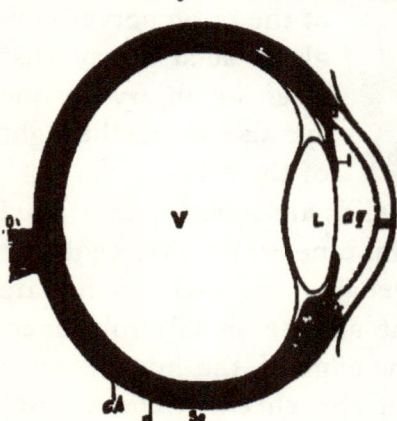

FIG. 81.—SECTION OF EYEBALL.

Sc.—Sclerotic coat. Co.—Cornea.
Ch.—Choroid coat. I.—Iris.
R.—Retina. V.—Vitreous humor.
L.—Crystalline lens. Aq.—Aqueous humor.

far from the lens do not appear distinct. If we wish these objects to be more distinct, we must use a thinner lens for near objects, and a thicker one for more distant ones, or change the position of the lens to conform with the distance of each object. In the eye, the rays of light from an object pass through the crystalline lens, which is a double convex lens (see definition), and an image is formed upon the retina. The crystalline lens is supplied with a small muscle, which makes

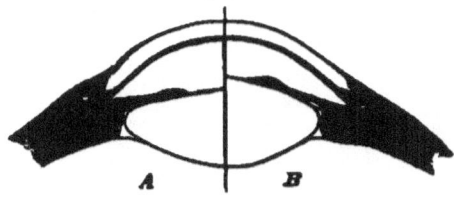

FIG. 89.—ACCOMMODATION.
A.—Lens adjusted for near objects.
B.—Lens adjusted for far objects.

it thicker or thinner as is necessary, thus adjusting the eye to far or to near objects. When the image is formed upon the retina an impression is produced which is transmitted to the brain by the optic nerve. This constitutes the act of seeing. The power which the lens possesses of becoming thicker or thinner, thus adjusting the eye to far or near objects, is called accommodation. Any interference with this accommodation hinders correct sight.

174. Near-sightedness and Far-sightedness.—To form a distinct image on a screen you must have the screen at the proper distance from the lens; if it be either too far from it or too near it the image will appear indistinct. In the well-formed natural eye, the retina, which is the screen, is just the right distance from the crystalline lens, and all images are distinct. In some people, however, the eyeball is longer from the front backward than it should be, and therefore the retina lies too far from the lens (see Fig. 83). In this case distant objects cannot be distinctly seen, and the person has what is called near-sightedness. If, as sometimes happens, a person's eyeballs are shorter than they should be, the retina is drawn too close to the lens. In such cases far objects are distinctly seen, but near objects are indistinct. This is what is called far-sightedness. In old age the crystal-

A —Normal Eye.
　　X.—Correct place for image or focus.

B.—Near Sight.
　　X.—Where image is formed.

C.—Far Sight.
　　X.—Where image is formed.

Fig 83.—Diagram to Illustrate Near-Sightedness and Far-Sightedness.

line lens becomes more or less hardened, and loses its power of accommodation, and the eyesight is thus made imperfect.

All these troubles in the sight can be remedied to a great extent by the use of glasses, the shape of which should vary, according to the trouble which they are intended to remedy.

175. The Iris.—The iris is a delicate curtain with a circular opening in its center. It is of different colors in different individuals, and hence we say of one person that he has blue eyes, of another that he has gray eyes, etc. The circular opening in the iris is called the *pupil.* It is placed immediately in front of the center of the crystalline lens, and thus by admitting the rays of light only at that point, prevents the image, which falls upon the retina, from being blurred, as would otherwise be the case.

Another important use of the iris is to regulate the amount of light admitted into the eye. All the light that enters the eye enters through the pupil. Too much light irritates the retina; hence, to prevent the entrance of too much or too strong light the iris contracts, and the pupil becomes smaller. If there is too little light the iris relaxes, and the pupil grows larger, thus allowing the entrance of more light. The peculiar action of the iris may be clearly illustrated by observing the eye of a cat.

176. Color-Blindness.—The perfect or normal eye is so constituted that its possessor is able readily to distinguish between different colors. Sometimes a person's eyes are in such a condition that they do not give the power of distinguishing colors, especially the difference between red and green. This condition is called color-blindness. Occasionally, color-blindness is such as to prevent the appreciation of any color, all colors appearing simply as shades.

177. Why we see an Object Single.—It would seem that as we have two eyes everything we look at would appear double. The reason that this is not the case is that the eyes are kept in such a position by the muscles of the eyeball as to cause the image to fall upon exactly the same place on both retinas. If the eyes are not so arranged, the image falls at different points on the two retinas, and we see double. This is what is called double vision.

178. Directions for the Care of the Eyes. — The eye is the most delicate and complicated organ of the body, and, therefore, requires the greatest care. It is liable to many diseases, and for any of these the advice of a trustworthy physician ought always to be sought.

Should any object enter the eye by accident, it should be at once removed, for if allowed to remain it may cause serious inflammation. Try to wash it out with water, and if this is found to be impossible, consult a physician. If lime or alkali should enter the eyes, wash them out quickly with a weak solution of vinegar, and bathe them freely with water.

If the eyes become painful and irritated from exposure to cold or from overwork, rest and frequent bathing with tepid or hot water will often afford complete relief.

Proper care of the eyes is most important to good eyesight. Avoid looking too long at distant or small objects. Never read or write by a feeble or unsteady light.

Do not read by a light which shines directly into the eyes, but turn your back to the light, allowing it to shine over the shoulder upon the paper or book. Reading while riding on the cars is hurtful to the eyesight. If the eyes become tired easily, or ache frequently, an eye specialist should be consulted.

Avoid using eye-washes or salves unless advised to do so by your physician. Such things often cause serious irritation and inflammation of the eyes.

179. Effects of Tobacco on the Eyes.—Tobacco has very injurious effects upon the eyes. It is a frequent cause of color-blindness. The irritating action of tobacco smoke causes haziness, and sometimes produces a total loss of the sight. Tobacco sometimes produces a wasting away of the optic nerve, and this leads, sooner or later, to partial or total blindness. This disease of the eye is called *tobacco-amaurosis*, and the peculiar symptoms which accompany it very clearly indicate tobacco as its principal cause.

180. Effects of Alcohol on the Sense of Sight.—The use of alcohol is responsible for many painful and serious diseases of the eyes. The blood-shot, inflamed condition of the eyeballs in confirmed alcohol drinkers shows that the eyes are very easily affected by this poison. Nearly all such persons are troubled, sooner or later, with disordered eyesight.

Drinkers of alcohol find it difficult to recover from diseases of the eye, especially if these diseases be of an inflammatory nature. The constant congestion which alcohol produces acts as a prevention to recovery, often hastening and rendering serious what might otherwise have been a slight and temporary disease.

Acute eyesight is absent in persons who indulge in alcohol, and the eyes of these persons easily tire with moderate work. Color-blindness and haziness of vision are of common occurrence among them, and indeed it is rarely that this class of people have normal, healthy eyes and eyesight.

CHAPTER XIX.

HEARING.

181. Sound.—Every movement of matter causes vibrations, or waves, in the air surrounding it. This being appreciated by the mind, produces the sensation of sound; and the appreciation of this sensation constitutes what is called hearing.

182. The Ear.—The ear is the organ by which we are enabled to hear. It consists of three parts:—

(1) The external ear;

(2) The middle ear;

(3) The internal ear, or labyrinth.

183. The External Ear.—The appearance of the external ear is too well known to need any minute description. It is composed of cartilage, covered with skin. Attached to it are three small muscles, which are so slightly developed in man as to be useless, but in many animals they are fully

Fig. 84.—The External Ear.

developed, causing the ear to be freely movable. From the external ear a canal or opening extends inward for about one and a quarter inches, being closed at its inner extremity by a thin membrane, called the *drum* of the ear, or the *membrane of the tympanum*.

in this canal there are several small glands, which secrete a waxy substance called the *cerumen*, or ear-wax; and from the walls of the canal grow short, stiff hairs, the object of which is to prevent the entrance of insects and foreign bodies into the inner ear.

184. The Middle Ear.—Just within the drum of the ear is a small, irregularly-shaped cavity, called the *tympanum*, or middle ear. Opening into the middle ear is a small tube, called the *eustachian tube*, which leads to the upper part of the throat.

This tube allows the air to pass in and out of the middle ear. Within this tympanum, or middle ear, there is a chain of very small bones, three in number. One of them is attached to the drum of the ear, another to a membrane of the internal ear, and the third lies between these two. The middle ear is separated from the internal ear by means of a thin, delicate membrane.

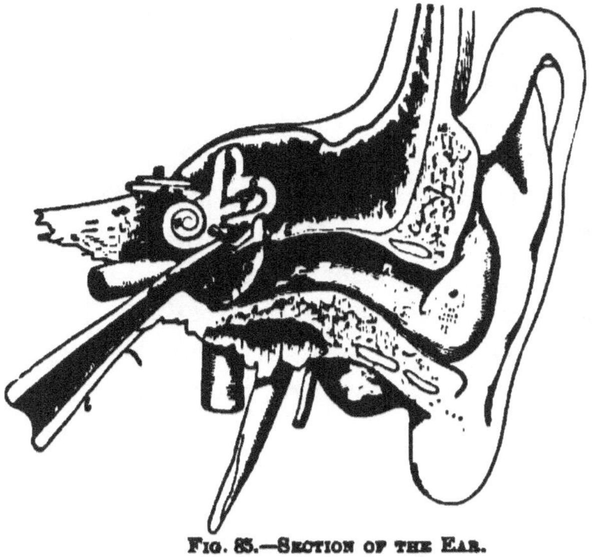

185. The Internal Ear.—The internal ear is a cavity, very irregular in shape and very complicated in structure. It is, in large part, made up of spiral tubes

FIG. 85.—SECTION OF THE EAR.

n.—Auditory canal.
o.—Drum of the ear.
p.—Tympanum or middle ear.

1, 2, 3.—Bones of the ear.
4, 5, 6, 7.—Internal ear.
8.—Auditory nerve.
b.—Eustachian tube.

which open into a sort of a cavity called the *vestibule*. The internal ear is filled with a watery fluid, and in its walls branches of the nerve of hearing are distributed. The nerve of hearing is called the *auditory nerve.*

186. The Act of Hearing.—The way we hear is as follows: The vibrations of the air, or the sound-waves strike upon the external ear, are collected by it, and sent through the canal to the drum of the ear. The sound-waves striking upon this drum cause it to vi‑ brate. This vibration is carried to the chain of bones in the tympanum, and thence to the liquid in the internal ear, finally producing certain impressions upon the fine nerves of hearing. These impressions are conveyed to the brain, and are there appreciated as sound.

187. Diseases and Injuries of the Ear.—Catarrh often causes deafness by the inflammation spreading from the throat to the ear through the eustachian tube. The drum of the ear sometimes becomes broken by violence, and deafness results. The hearing may often be affected by sudden loud noises, or by the introduction of foreign objects into the ear. Cold in the head is a very common cause of partial deafness.

188. Effects of Alcohol and Tobacco on the Hearing.—The habitual use of alcohol often causes a congestion of the throat, which, extending through the eustachian tube, affects the hearing.

The use of tobacco, especially the smoking of it, often leads to congestion of the internal ear. Snuff-taking is very harmful, and should never be indulged in. Persons who are habitual users of tobacco, very rarely have an acute sense of hearing.

CHAPTER XX

SMELLING—TASTING—FEELING.

189. The Sense of Smell.—The organ of the sense of smell is the nose. The mucous membrane which lines the nasal passages, is supplied with filaments, or branches of the *olfactory nerve*, which is the nerve of smell. These filaments enter the nose through a sieve-like bone in the roof of the nasal cavity. The most common theory concerning this subject is that every object which has odorous properties gives off invisible particles, and these particles, coming in contact with the nerve filaments in the nose, produce a peculiar sensation. This sensation, when appreciated by the brain, is called smell.

FIG. 86.—SECTION OF THE NOSE.
(Showing the Branches of the Olfactory Nerve.)

If one would properly enjoy the sense of smell, the lining membrane of the nose must always be kept in a healthy condition. Colds in the head should not be neglected, and irritating substances ought never to be inhaled. The object of the sense of smell is to enable us to distinguish fit articles of food, and to warn us of poisonous or impure air.

190. The Sense of Taste.—The sense of taste lies in the tongue and the upper part of the throat. A substance to have taste must be soluble, so that it may be partially absorbed by the mucous membrane which lines these parts, and thus come into contact with the nerves of taste, which are distributed there.

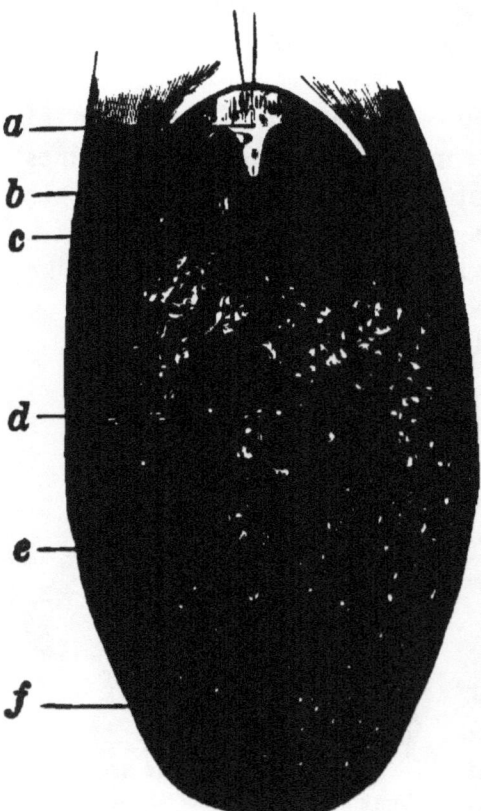

FIG. 87.—THE HUMAN TONGUE.
(Showing also the back part of the mouth.)
a.—The palate.　　c.—Epiglottis.
b.—Tonsil.　　d, e, f.—Papillæ.

The tongue is covered with small elevations, called *papillæ*, and it is in these papillæ that most of the nerves of taste are situated. Different parts of the tongue perceive and convey the sensation of different tastes —as bitter, sweet, sour, salty, etc. Both the sense of taste and that of smell are exercised when eating or drinking such substances as have an aroma. This explains why the taste of many articles resembles their odor.

The nerves of taste are in close sympathy with the

stomach, and often tell us that the stomach will rebel against certain articles of food. Taste enables us to distinguish between wholesome and unwholesome foods. By taste, flavors are appreciated, and these when pleasant, stimulate the flow of the saliva and gastric juice, and thus aid in the digestion of the various foods.

191. The Sense of Touch.—The sense of touch is located in the skin, and in some of the mucous membranes. The skin is covered with minute elevations, or papillæ, and in these the nerves of touch are distributed. The sense of touch enables us to appreciate pain, heat, cold, roughness, hardness, and other qualities of different substances. The sense of touch in the tip of the tongue and the tips of the fingers is very acute. The sense of touch is relied upon in all acts and movements of the body. It acts as the safeguard of the body.

192. Effects of Alcohol and Tobacco on these Senses.—The use of alcohol and tobacco tends to blunt all the senses, and to weaken the action of all the nerves of sensation. It especially interferes with the sense of smell, often completely destroying it. Alcohol causes congestion and thickening of the mucous membrane of the nose, thus paralyzing, to a certain extent, the nerves of smell. The sense of taste is blunted by the use of alcohol or tobacco. The persistent smoking of tobacco often renders a person almost totally incapable of distinguishing flavors. Alcohol and tobacco both benumb the nervous system. The sense of feeling, as well as the delicacy of touch, is frequently blunted. If alcohol is taken in large quantities, it causes unconsciousness and complete insensibility to pain or touch.

FIRST SUPPLEMENTARY CHAPTER.

CARE OF THE SICK ROOM.

If you have a sick friend or relative, and would have him recover his health in the least possible time, you should see that proper care is taken of his sick room.

193. Air.—Fresh air and sunlight are direct enemies to disease, so see to it that the patient has both. His room should be on the sunny side of the house, where the cheerful sunlight can be allowed to pour into it. Sunlight kills disease germs, but darkness breeds them. A light and cheerful room will hasten recovery, but a dark and cheerless one will retard it.

Plenty of fresh air is of the utmost importance. Have an open fire-place in the room if possible. It not, then see that the windows and doors are opened enough to supply an abundance of fresh air. If the patient be protected from a draught by the use of extra blankets, the room may frequently be aired out.

194. Furniture in the Room.—The less furniture the better. Have the floor bare, with rugs or strips of carpet placed upon it to deaden the sound when walking. Have hard-bottomed chairs; upholstered ones are not suitable for a sick room.

195. Noise.—Have a care not to wear squeaky shoes when entering the room; and see that the hinges of the doors do not creak.

Do not allow any unnecessary noise in or near the

room, for sick persons are easily disturbed and annoyed. Do not allow visitors to enter the room except in cases of necessity.

Never converse in whispers in the presence of the patient, but carry on all your conversation in the natural tone of voice. Do not converse with the sick person so much as to tire him, nor allow others to do so.

196. Medicines.—Keep the medicines out of sight, and do not allow drinking-water to stand in the room, but always supply fresh water when it is required. Have all the medicines properly labeled, so that no mistake will be made in giving them. Be very careful to give them punctually at the time designated by the physician.

197. Cleanliness. — Keep the bed fresh and clean, and the room likewise. All soiled clothing should be removed from the room at once and placed in boiling water. Never neglect cleanliness.

198. Temperature.—Keep the temperature of the room as nearly uniform as possible; usually a temperature of 70° or 75° is advisable. Avoid the admission of sudden draughts of cold air; and, with equal care, avoid making the room so warm as to induce languor.

199. The Physician.—Above all things, obey the orders of the attending physician and never give to the patient this, that, or the other thing which kind neighbors may recommend as being useful, or as having cured some one else of the same disease.

By giving heed to the above suggestions you will add greatly to the comfort of your friend or relative, and assist in promoting his speedy recovery. Always remember that these five things are necessary in the sick room; light, cleanliness, fresh air, quiet, and cheerfulness.

SECOND SUPPLEMENTARY CHAPTER.

WHAT TO DO IN EMERGENCIES.

The following hints are intended to give you an idea of what to do in certain cases, " until the doctor comes." Never attempt to treat a severe injury, or an acute disease yourself. Always send for a physician, and until he arrives, follow any hints you may derive from the following suggestions:

200. Accidents.—In all cases of accident, the first thing to do is to see that a crowd does not gather closely about the victim. A space should be left clear about him of at least eight or ten feet on every side. Send immediately for a physician. If the victim be unconscious, or in a faint, lay him flat on his back, with his arms and hands extended. This gives his heart a chance to act without interference. At the same time loosen his clothing about his neck and chest, and remove anything which may interfere with the flow of blood toward the head. If the person be but slightly injured, he will probably begin to recover soon after you have given him a sip of water, and have bathed his face and forehead with water, and, perhaps, have held a little ammonia near his nostrils.

By the time you have done all this, a physician will likely have arrived, and all further examination and treatment should be left to him.

201. Drowning.—Drowning is a form of asphyxia. After the body of a drowned person is recovered from the water, the face should be turned downwards, and the tongue pressed down, so that any water or mucus which may be in the throat may be removed. Then persistently perform artificial respiration, as explained on page 82, at the same time rubbing the extremities with the dry hands, and applying hot flannels to the body. After the patient has begun to recover, keep him warm and quiet for quite a while. In asphyxia from strangling, suffocation by gases, etc., carry out the same plan of treatment.

202. Sunstroke.—In cases of sunstroke, place the person attacked in a cool, airy place. Do not allow a crowd to collect closely about him. Remove his clothing, and lay him flat on his back. Dash him all over with cold water—ice-water, if it can be obtained—and rub the entire body with pieces of ice. This treatment is used to reduce the heat of the body, for in all cases of sunstroke the temperature of the body is greatly increased. When the body has become cooler, wipe it dry, and remove the person to a dry locality. If respiration ceases, or becomes exeeedingly slow, practice artificial respiration, as on page 82. After the patient has apparently recovered, he should be kept quiet in bed for some time.

203. Burns and Scalds.—If the clothing of a person catches fire, throw him on the ground, and instantly wrap his body up in a carpet, rug, overcoat, or anything that will serve to smother the flames and keep them from the face. If a burn is very slight, a constant application of cold water is sufficient treatment. After

11

the pain has disappeared, apply lard or vaseline to the parts. Very useful applications to a burned surface are: linseed oil and lime-water, olive oil, flour, white of an egg, and a lather of soapsuds. If a burn be severe, leave all further treatment to a reliable physician.

204. Bruises.—In bruises of a moderate kind, the best treatment is to elevate the part affected, and then to apply to it ice, or cold, wet cloths. If the person become chilled, discontinue the cold applications, and keep the injured part perfectly clean and dry. Keep the part perfectly quiet until the soreness and swelling have disappeared.

205. Cuts.—In cuts, if the bleeding be profuse, check it by the methods given on page 65, for checking hemorrhage. Then draw the edges of the wound together and secure them there by a bandage, or by strips of adhesive plaster. Do not change the dressings on a cut too often, but when you do change them, see that the cut is washed perfectly clean before renewing them.

206. Frost-bite.—Frost-bite is caused by exposure to intense cold. It usually attacks the nose, ears, fingers, or toes. When a part of the body becomes frost-bitten, do not enter a warm room, or make warm applications. Briskly rub the part with snow, or apply ice-water to it until the circulation of blood is started in it. Do not even then hold a frost-bitten part of the body near the fire. If the itching and burning is severe, bathe the part in cold water, or apply some simple ointment to it. If the frost-bite is severe, always consult your physician in regard to it.

207. Choking.—Choking occurs from the lodging of a foreign body in the throat. Quite often a sharp blow with the hand between the shoulders will serve to dislodge it. If not, then have the person open the mouth widely, and by pressing the tongue down, you may be able to see the foreign substance, and to remove it. If this cannot be done, have the choking person drink water, and swallow mashed potatoes, or something of that kind, so that, if possible, the substance may be forced down into the stomach. If none of these bring relief, then produce vomiting by giving to the person copious draughts of warm salt-water, or warm water in which mustard has been mixed.

208. Croup.—Croup usually begins somewhat suddenly, and if severe, a physician should at once be sent for. In the meanwhile, try to induce vomiting by tickling the throat, or with a teaspoonful of syrup of ipecac repeated every ten or fifteen minutes. Then keep the throat well wrapped in hot, wet cloths, and allow the person affected to breathe steam.

209. Sore Throat.— There are many kinds of sore throat, and some of them are very serious; hence, it is always advisable that a physician should be consulted. A gargle of salt and water, or of a solution of chlorate of potash, or of salt-petre is useful in relieving a sore throat. Applications of salt pork, lard, or vaseline on a rough piece of flannel, will also aid in its recovery.

210. Foreign Bodies in the Eye.—Nature's method of removing foreign bodies from the eye, is to wash them out by an increased secretion of tears. Sometimes washing the eye freely with warm water will answer the purpose. A very useful way of removing bodies from the inside of the upper eyelid is as follows : Separate the eyelid from the eyeball by pulling upon the eyelashes, then draw the upper lid down over the lower one, and allow it to move back to its natural place. The lashes of the lower lid thus act as a brush on the inner surface of the upper lid. If the foreign body can be seen, it can generally be removed by brushing it with the corner of a handkerchief. If these means fail consult a physician.

211. Poisons.—A person may be poisoned by acids, alkalis, arsenic, opium, aconite, strychnine, etc.

The first thing to do in all cases of poisoning is to empty the stomach. This may be done by giving to the person a warm and strong solution of salt, or a teacupful of warm water into which a teaspoonful of ground mustard has been stirred. Tickling the throat with the finger or a feather will often produce vomiting. After vomiting has been induced, give to the patient a quantity of milk and white of egg, mixed with water, to drink. If the poison is such as to injure and inflame the stomach, give barley-water, olive oil, etc. By this time a physician will have arrived, and can carry out any further treatment required.

212. Poisonous Bites and Stings.—If a person has been bitten by an animal supposed to be mad, or by a snake, tie a bandage about the limb directly above the wound. Apply suction to the wound until the blood flows freely; then wash it out and paint it with tincture of iodine or. nitrate of silver, or burn it with the red-hot end of some pointed instrument, as a knitting needle. In case of a sting by a bee or other insect, pull the sting from the wound, if it has been left there, and rub the part with a strong solution of soda, or of salt; or, if these are not at hand, a coating of mud will help allay the pain.

THIRD SUPPLEMENTARY CHAPTER.

CONTAGIOUS OR COMMUNICABLE DISEASES—HOW SPREAD AND HOW PREVENTED.

213. The Germ Theory of Disease.—By contagious diseases we understand those diseases which are communicated from one person to another, either by direct contact or by breathing air rendered impure by such persons. All contagious diseases are caused by certain specific microscopic bodies or organisms called " germs." Each disease has its own peculiar germ, and if such germ finds its way into the body of a person, under certain conditions, it will produce in that person the disease of which it is the peculiar germ. These germs may be carried from one person to another in several different ways. They are exceedingly small. Some float with minute particles of dust in the air, and may thus be breathed into the lungs, or may find lodgment in some part of the body where the skin or mucous membrane is broken; some find their way into the body by being in the water which is drunk, or the food which is eaten. If such a thing could be possible as to kill all these germs, then contagious diseases would cease to exist; but as such is not possible, it is our duty to do all in our power to prevent the spreading of the germs and consequently the increase of the diseases which they produce. Vast numbers of deaths occur every year from contagious diseases, and certainly with due precautions and care this death rate could be greatly reduced.

The principal diseases which we may class as contagious or communicable diseases are consumption, diphtheria, typhoid fever, scarlet fever, smallpox, measles, whooping cough, and, perhaps, pneumonia. Let us, so far as our space will permit, endeavor to learn how these diseases are spread and what measures should be taken to prevent their increase.

214. Consumption.—Phthisis or consumption is a disease of the lungs, and a most dreaded disease. More persons die of consumption than of any other disease, hence the importance of its prevention cannot be over-estimated. The germs which cause consumption are called *bacilli* (see Definition, p. 181). They exist in great numbers in the sputum (see Definition, p. 189) of consumptive persons. When this sputum becomes dry it is easily converted into dust, and thus floats in the air, carrying the germs with it, to be breathed by other persons. The only way, therefore, of preventing the spread of these germs is by the immediate and total destruction of the sputum of consumptive persons. Such persons should never expectorate upon the streets and sidewalks, or upon the floors of street cars or other conveyances, for the sputum becoming dry and mixing with the dust is carried and spread by the air. The best precaution that all who have a cough can take is to carry pieces of cloth to receive the sputum, which cloths should be at once put into a paper or a rubber bag, and then the whole be burned at the first opportunity. A consumptive person should always sleep alone, and the utmost care should be taken to keep his room well aired and scrupulously clean. Consumption is now known to be a contagious and communicable disease.

215. Diphtheria.—This dreaded disease is communicated by the saliva and excretions from the throat. By the drying of the excretions, a fine dust is formed which floats in the air and is breathed by other persons. Poor drainage and sewerage, no doubt, cause many cases of diphtheria. It should be remembered, that the diphtheria germs often remain in the throat many days after the patient has apparently recovered. To prevent the spread of this disease every one who is suffering from it should be at once isolated, and all clothing and articles of furniture used by him should be thoroughly disinfected before coming in contact with any other person. For several days after the patient has apparently recovered, he should remain isolated, and not be permitted to mingle with others until all possible danger of infection is removed.

216. Typhoid Fever.—This disease is rarely contracted immediately from the patient by being in his company, but is contracted from the germs arising from the discharges of the person. It is frequently caused by germs contained in the water which one drinks. If there is the least doubt as to the purity of water, such water should be well boiled before being used for drinking purposes, as boiling kills the typhoid germs. Drainage and sewerage should be well looked after, and all clothing and discharges of a typhoid patient should be destroyed or thoroughly disinfected.

217. Scarlet Fever.—This disease is very easily contracted, and is very contagious. The scarlet fever germ is present in the discharges of the nose and throat, and especially in the small scales which occur on the surface of the skin during the progress of the disease. To prevent the spread of this disease the patient should be isolated, and all clothing, etc., be thoroughly disinfected. This same rule applies to cases of smallpox, measles, and whooping cough.

218. General Precautions.—No person who has been exposed to any contagious disease should be allowed to mingle with other persons, especially children, until it is certain as to whether such person is infected with the disease. No one should go from a sick room to children, or other persons, until he has changed his clothing, and thoroughly washed his face, head, and hands. The clothing of a diseased person should never be worn by any one else, and none of his bed clothing should be used until thoroughly disinfected. It is always best not to go near a sick person unless you are absolutely needed there, and never should the lips be touched to cups, spoons, food, or drink, which have been in the sick room or which the sick person has handled. After the sick person has recovered, every thing that has touched him or was in his room, should be burned or thoroughly disinfected. Perfect cleanliness of houses, food and water is necessary to the prevention of the spread of contagious diseases, as is also the utmost care in keeping away from sick persons, and those who have been exposed to disease.

219. Effects of Alcohol in Contagious Diseases.—Alcohol drinkers, in contagious diseases as well as in other diseases, can scarcely hope for speedy recovery. Their general health has been undermined by this poison, and the consequence is that they are not in a proper condition to combat any disease. The muscular system has been weakened, the nervous system is unstrung, the circulatory system does not act right, and the digestive system is wholly unable to perform its proper work. If a person is in this condition, it is easy to understand why he is not only very liable to contract disease, and especially one of the contagious diseases, but also why he cannot expect to recover as soon as persons who do not indulge in alcoholic drinks. The generally exhausted condition of the alcohol drinker explains all this. Many a man has died of disease, who, if he had not been an alcohol drinker, would probably have recovered and lived many years. Disease seems especially likely to attack persons who are drinkers of alcohol, and disease germs seem to find in such persons a congenial soil for their growth and development. With these facts before us, why should we not say that one very important precaution to be taken, in order to prevent the spread of contagious diseases, is always to let alcoholic drinks absolutely alone?

220. Alcohol in Hereditary Diseases.—Children of parents addicted to the alcohol habit have often an uncontrollable appetite for strong drinks. This appetite must be considered as nothing more nor less than a disease, the result of inheritance. This, however, is not the only disease which drunken parents transmit to their offspring. Statistics show conclusively that a large proportion of persons afflicted with insanity are the descendants of alcohol drinkers; they show also that the children of intemperate persons are frequently predisposed to epilepsy, or fits; and that in very many cases of idiocy, one or both of the parents were addicted to drink, and the deprivation of intellect was directly traceable to the alcohol habit.

QUESTIONS FOR REVIEWS AND EXAMINATIONS.

INTRODUCTION.

Define physiology. What other studies are closely allied to it? Define anatomy. What is hygiene? What important facts do physiology, anatomy, and hygiene teach us? Why is it important that we understand these studies?

CHAPTER I.

What is the color of bone? What are the properties of bone? What are the uses of bone? How many tissues exist in bone? What are these tissues called? What are their uses? Of what is bone composed? Which part gives bone its hardness? Which gives it its elasticity? By what experiments are the parts composing bone separated? What is the difference in the bones of the young and of the old? What is the character of bone in very young infants? When do one's bones reach their full development? What is the periosteum? What are its uses? What diseases and injuries of bones are common? What are the effects of alcohol and tobacco on the bones?

CHAPTER II.

What is the skeleton? How many bones are there in the human skeleton? How are they united to one another? What are ligaments? What structures form the human skeleton? How are the bones classified?

What are the uses of these classes? How many groups of bones are there? What is the skull? What is the cranium? How are the bones of the skull united? What is a suture? How many bones are in the face? How many of these are movable? What is the trunk? What is the spinal column? Of what is it composed? Describe a vertebra. How are the vertebræ attached to each other? What is the use of the backbone? What is the chest? What is the abdomen? What are the bones of the chest? What is the pelvis? Describe the bones of the upper extremities. Describe the bones of the lower extremities. What is the appearance of the ends of the long bones?

CHAPTER III.

What is a joint? How many kinds of joints are there? What are movable joints? How is a joint lubricated? Name the principal kinds of movable joints. Give examples. What diseases and injuries of joints are common?

CHAPTER IV.

What are tissues? What is fibrous tissue? Fatty tissue? Bony tissue? Describe the formation of muscular tissue. How many classes of muscles are there? Describe each. How are muscles attached? How do they act? How many muscles are there in the human body? How do they vary in size and shape? What important properties do muscles possess? What are the muscles of expression? What are those of mastication? Describe the muscles of the trunk; of the upper extremities; of the lower extremities. What are the effects of alcohol on the muscles? Of tobacco?

CHAPTER V.

How may muscles be developed? What change takes place in a muscle which is not used? How should exercise be taken? What are the results of excessive exercise? Of what uses are indoor exercises? How should they be practiced? What are the effects of alcohol upon muscular development?

CHAPTER VI.

How is bodily nutrition carried on? What is the blood? About how much blood exists in the human body? How is the blood carried to different parts of the body? What is the composition of blood? What is the plasma? Of what use is it? How much of the blood is made up of blood corpuscles? How many kinds of blood corpuscles are there? Which is the most abundant? What are the uses of the blood? What is oxygen? What is carbonic acid? What has the blood to do with these two substances? What are the uses of the white blood corpuscles? What is coagulation? What is a clot? What are the effects of alcohol on the blood? What effect does tobacco have on the blood?

CHAPTER VII.

What is meant by the circulation of the blood? What are the organs of circulation? What is the heart? How is it held in position? What is the pericardium? How many cavities are in the heart? What are they called? Which have the thickest walls? How many valves are in the heart? What are their uses? Where are they situated? Of what are they composed? What large blood-vessels open into the heart? Describe the action of the heart. How often does the heart contract? What are the sounds of the heart? What causes them? How may it be told if the valves of the heart are in good condition or not? What nerves are supplied to the heart? What effect do they have on the heart's action? What is the pulse? How can you feel it? What will cause it to be more rapid? What is the capacity of the heart? What are arteries? What is the largest artery of the body? What are capillaries? What are veins? How do veins differ from arteries? What are the effects of alcohol on the organs of circulation?

CHAPTER VIII.

Describe the course of the circulation. What is the color of the pure blood? Of the impure? What effect has exercise upon the circulation? What disorders of the circulation often occur? What are the causes of these disorders? What is hemorrhage? How may it be checked? What is fainting? What should be done with a fainting person? What are the effects of alcohol on the circulation?

CHAPTER IX.

What are the organs of respiration? What is the respiratory tract? Describe the nasal passages. Why should you breathe through the nose? What is the pharynx? What is the larynx? What is the glottis? What are the vocal cords? What is the trachea? How is it lined? What helps it to keep its circular shape during the act of breathing? What are the bronchial tubes? Describe the lungs. What is the pleura? What are

air-cells ? Of what are their walls principally composed ?
What are the muscles of respiration ? Which is the
principal one ? What effects do alcohol and tobacco
have on the organs of respiration ?

CHAPTER X.

How do we breathe ? What is inspiration ? What
is expiration ? How often does a person breathe ?
What is the total capacity of the lungs ? How much air
is taken into the lungs in ordinary inspiration ? Give
some examples of modified respiration. What is the
air ? What is the most important part of the air ?
What is carbonic acid ? Is it poisonous ? What test
should be used where its presence is suspected ? What
are the objects of respiration ? What changes take
place in the blood during respiration ? What change
occurs in the air ? What is the character of air when it
leaves the lungs ? How may the air become impure ?
What is ventilation ? What is the object of ventilation ? Describe the principles of ventilation. What
is asphyxia ? From what causes may it occur ? What
is necessary to restore an asphyxiated person ? Describe artificial respiration. How long should artificial
respiration be practiced on an asphyxiated person ?
What are the effects of alcohol on respiration ?

CHAPTER XI.

Do the tissues of the body ever wear out ? What
becomes of them ? What is assimilation ? What is
hunger ? How may it be satisfied ? What is thirst ?
How may it be satisfied ? What kind of food is neces-

sary to proper nutrition? Do all tissues require the same kind of nourishment? What is food? How are foods classified? What three classes of principles exist in food? What is the most important inorganic principle of food? Name some other inorganic principles. What are organic nitrogenized principles of food? What are the principal foods of this class? Which is capable of sustaining life of itself? Where are these principles found? What foods belong to the organic non-nitrogenized class? Where does sugar occur? Where are the fats found? Where is starch found? Of what use to the body are these principles supposed to be? What are drinks? What is the basis of all drinks? What kind of water should be used for drinking? If water be suspected of being impure, what should be done with it? How much water does the system require each day? What is alcohol? What are alcoholic drinks? Name some alcoholic drinks. Do they quench the thirst? Do they benefit the system? What effects do alcoholic drinks have upon the system? Do they aid in bodily nutrition?

CHAPTER XII.

What is the object of digestion? What is the digestive canal? Of what does it consist? Describe the course the food follows when taken into the body. What is the object of chewing the food? What is mastication? What are the organs of mastication? How many teeth are there? Describe the construction of a tooth. How are the teeth classified? What work does each class perform? How many jaws are there? Are they movable? What is the saliva? From where does

the saliva come? What is the parotid gland? Where
are the salivary glands situated? What is the object of
the saliva? What is the esophagus? Where does the
food pass when it is swallowed? What are the effects
of alcohol and tobacco on mastication?

CHAPTER XIII.

Describe the stomach. What is its capacity? What
openings has it? Of what are its walls chiefly composed? With what is it lined? What are the peptic
glands? What is the gastric juice? What class of food
is digested in the stomach? Describe the action of the
stomach during digestion. How long does it take food
to be digested in the stomach? What care and precautions should be taken in eating? Why should our
meals be at regular intervals? What are the effects of
alcohol on the stomach? What are the effects of
tobacco on the stomach? What diseases of the stomach
are common?

CHAPTER XIV.

What becomes of the food which is not digested in
the stomach? What is the chyme? With what fluids
does it come in contact in the small intestine? What
is the small intestine? What is the duodenum? What
ducts open into it? Describe the liver. What digestive
fluid is secreted by the liver? What is bile? What is
its action in digestion? What is jaundice? Describe
the pancreas. What digestive fluid does it secrete?
What action has this fluid in digestion? What are the
effects of alcohol on the liver? What is absorption?
How is the food absorbed? How does absorption take

place in the small intestine? What are the lacteals? What are the intestinal villi? What substance is chiefly absorbed by the villi? What are the lymphatics? Describe the thoracic duct.

CHAPTER XV.

What is the skin? What are the uses of the skin? Of how many layers does the skin consist? Describe each layer. What gives color to the skin? What are the hair and the nails? Describe a hair. Describe a nail. What are the uses of the hair and the nails? What is perspiration? What amount of perspiration is secreted by the skin? What is the object of perspiration? What glands are found in the skin? What is the object of each? What are the effects of alcohol on the skin? Name some common injuries to the skin. How would you treat such injuries?

CHAPTER XVI.

Why is cleanliness of the skin necessary? What is the proper way to keep the skin clean? What kind of a bath is most strengthening? What precautions should be observed when a warm bath is taken? When should a bath be taken? How often? What kind of clothing is most comfortable in winter? In summer?

CHAPTER XVII.

What is the nervous system? What are its objects? What two great nerve-systems are there? Of what does nerve-tissue consist? What office do nerve-cells perform? Nerve-fibers? What is a nerve center?

What are nerves? What two kind of nerve-fibers form the nerves? Give an example of their action. What constitutes a nerve current? What is the rapidity of a nerve current? Name a few varieties of motor and sensory nerves. Of what does the sympathetic nerve system consist? How many ganglions are there? What part of the body does this system supply? Of what does the cerebro-spinal system consist? What part of the body does this system supply? What is the brain? Of what is it composed? What is its average weight? Describe its appearance. Describe the cerebrum. What are the functions of the cerebrum? What occurs if the cerebrum be removed from a bird? What occurs if the cerebrum be injured or diseased? Describe the cerebellum. What are its functions? What is the medulla oblongata? Describe it. What are its functions? What is the spinal cord? Describe it. How many nerves branch from it? What part of the body do they supply? What are the functions of the spinal cord and spinal nerves? What is "reflex action"? What effects do diseases or injuries of the spinal cord produce? What are the effects of alcohol on the brain? What are) the general effects of alcohol on the nervous system?

CHAPTER XVIII.

What are the special senses? What is the eye? Describe the eyeball. Of how many layers does its wall consist? What are these layers called? What is the vitreous humor? What is the iris? What is the crystalline lens? How is the eyeball moved? Describe the optic nerve. What are the eyelids? What glands are in the eyelids? What secretes the tears? How are the tears drained from the eye? What is near-sightedness? What is far-sightedness? How is each remedied? How is the amount of light admitted to the eyes regulated? What is color-blindness? How is it that we see objects single? What injuries to the eyes are common? What precautions should we take so as to preserve our eyesight? What are the effects of alcohol and tobacco on the eyes?

CHAPTER XIX.

What is sound? Of how many parts does the ear consist? Describe the external ear. What is the drum of the ear? What is the object of the short hairs in the ear? Describe the middle ear. What is it called? What is the eustachian tube? Describe the internal ear. What is the nerve of hearing? Describe the way in which we hear. What diseases and injuries of the ear are common? What are the effects of alcohol and tobacco on the hearing?

CHAPTER XX.

What is the organ of smell? How do we smell? What precautions are necessary to preserve a normal sense of smell? Where is the sense of taste situated? What are the papillæ of the tongue? Of what use is the sense of taste to us? Where is the sense of touch located? How are the nerves of touch distributed? In what part of the body is the sense of touch especially acute? What are the effects of alcohol and tobacco on the sense of smell? On the sense of taste? On the sense of touch?

DEFINITIONS.

abdo'men. The cavity of the trunk situated below the ribs and diaphragm. The name is also applied to the outside front portion of the trunk between the chest and the pelvis. See § 14.

albu'men. One of the most important food principles. See § 96. It is found in its purest natural form in the white of an egg.

al'cohol. A liquid formed by the fermentation of aqueous sugar-solutions, or by the destructive distillation of organic bodies. Throughout this book the word is used to include all liquors containing alcohol in any quantity, whether small or great. See §§ 9, 28, 39, 47, 62, 70, 78, 90, 99, 100, 110, etc.

al'coholic liquors. Liquors which contain alcohol in either small or large quantities, and are used as beverages. See § 9.

ale. Carefully made beer of a certain strength. See definition of *beer*, below.

anat'omy. The science which describes the bodily structure of animals or plants. *Human anatomy* is the science which describes the appearance and structure of the different parts of the human body. *Animal anatomy*, or *comparative anatomy*, relates to animals in general. *Vegetable anatomy* relates to plants.

aor'ta. The main artery in the body, from which all the other arteries (except the pulmonary) have their origin, either directly or indirectly. See § 53.

append'age. That which is attached to something as a necessary part of it. Thus the hair and nails are said to be appendages of the skin. See § 134.

a'queous hu'mor. The fluid which fills that portion of the eye between the cornea and the crystalline lens. See § 168.

ar'tery. One of a system of blood-vessels which conveys the blood from the heart to all parts of the body. The two principal arteries are the *aor'ta*, which rises from the left ventricle of the heart, and the *pul'monary artery*, which rises from the right ventricle. The former, with its branches, carries pure blood to all the tissues; the latter, with its branches, carries impure blood to the lungs, there to undergo purification. See § 59.

artifi'cial respira'tion. Breathing by artificial means. See § 89.

asphyxia (as fix'ia). A stoppage of the breath, as in choking, drowning, or paralysis of the muscles of respiration. See § 88.

assimila'tion. The process by which nutriment is changed into, and becomes part of, a living tissue. See § 91.

au'ditory nerve. The nerve of hearing. See § 185.

au'ricles. The two upper cavities of the heart into which the blood enters as it returns from the other parts of the body. See § 51.

bacil'li (ba sil'i). Microscopical vegetable organisms, having the form of very slender, straight filaments. A germ of the large class of micro-organisms known as *bacteria*. See § 213.

beer. An alcoholic liquor made generally from barley. The grain is first induced to sprout, thereby changing its starch into sugar. It is then ground, and its fermentable substance is extracted by hot water. It is then boiled with an infusion of hops, after which it is drawn off into vats, and suffered to ferment. After it has become clear it is put in barrels, or kegs, and stored away, or sent to market. The quality of the beer depends upon the length of time that it has been allowed to ferment. See definition of *fermentation*, below. See § 99.

ti'ceps. The large muscle on the front part of the arm below the shoulder. See § 24.

bile. A fluid secreted by the liver. See § 124.

blood. The fluid which circulates in the arteries and veins, carrying nutriment to all parts of the body, and assisting in the removal of useless and worn-out matter. See §§ 40–48.

cap'illaries. The smallest of the blood-vessels, connecting the veins and arteries. See § 60.

car'tilage. Gristle. An elastic animal tissue, similar to bone, but softer. See § 5.

casein (kā'sē in). A nitrogenous food principle, found abundantly in milk. See § 96.

catarrh (ka tar'). An inflammation, either acute or chronic, of the mucous membrane of some organ, usually of the nose or throat.

cerebel'lum. The little brain. The smaller and hinder division of the brain. See § 157.

cere'bro spi'nal sys'tem. That part of the nervous system which has its origin in the brain and spinal cord. See §§ 142–161.

cer'ebrum. The larger division of the brain. See § 154.

cerumen (se roo' men). The wax-like substance secreted in the passage of the external ear. See § 183.

chest. The cavity of the body above the diaphragm. See § 14.

chlo'ral (klō'ral). A narcotic compound, prepared from chlorine and alcohol. See § 166.

cho'roid coat (kō' roid). The middle coat of the eye. See §168.

chyle (kīle). The milky fluid found in the lacteals during the process of digestion. See § 129.

chyme (kime). The food as it passes into the small intestine after partial digestion in the stomach. See § 120.

ci'der. The juice of apples. *Sweet cider*, when first obtained from the apple, does not contain alcohol. By exposure to the air, it soon begins to ferment. *Hard cider* is that which, by fermentation, has lost its sweetness, and has become an alcoholic liquor. If the fermentation is suffered to continue, the alcohol is changed into acetic acid, and vinegar is produced. See definition of *fermentation*, below. See § 99.

congest'ed. Containing an unnatural accumulation of blood.

convolu'tions. The wave-like projections on the surface of the brain. See § 154.

co-or'dinate move'ments. The consistent and harmonious action of various parts, as of the muscles in walking, etc.

cor'puscles. Small bodies, usually too minute to be distinguished by the naked eye. See § 44.

circula'tion. The passage of the blood from the heart into all parts of the body, and its return to the heart. See §§ 64–70.

cir'culatory sys'tem. The heart and blood-vessels taken together as an assemblage of organs for the performance of a particular function. See §§ 49–63.

coagula'tion. The change of a liquid from the fluid form to a curdlike state, not by evaporation, but by some kind of chemical reaction. See § 46.

cor'nea. The transparent portion of the external coat of the eye. See § 169.

crys'talline lens. The lens of the eye, situated immediately behind the pupil. See §§ 168, 175.

cu'ticle. The outer layer of the skin. See § 133.

der'mis. The true skin, or inner layer of the skin. See § 133.

diaphragm (di'a fram). The membraneous muscle which separates the thoracic from the abdominal cavity. See § 80.

diges'tion. The process by which the food is prepared for absorption into the circulation. See §§ 102–125.

distillation. The process of obtaining the spirit or essence of a substance by evaporating it and then condensing it.

drum of the ear. The membrane between the external ear and the tympanum. See § 183.

duode'num (du o dē' num). The upper part of the small intestine, in which the bile and pancreatic juice come in contact with the food. See § 122.

elimina'tion. The process of removing or thrusting out.

enam'el. A dense, smooth, glistening substance which covers the crown of a tooth. See § 105.

epider'mis. The outer layer of the skin. See § 133.

epiglot'tis. The valve which prevents the entrance of food and drink into the larynx. See § 74.

esoph'agus. The canal through which food and drink pass into the stomach; the gullet. See § 109.

eustach'ian tube. The tube extending from the middle ear to the throat. See § 184.

excre'tion. The removal of useless or harmful substances. Also, any of these useless or harmful substances so removed.

faint'ing. See § 69.

fi'ber. A slender, thread-like element, as of any tissue.

fi'brous tis'sue. The connective tissue of different parts of the body, such as that composing the ligaments of joints, the tendons of muscles, etc. It is composed chiefly of white inelastic, or of yellow elastic fibers. See § 20.

fi'brin. A complex nitrogenous substance which appears in fresh blood, and is found in the chyle. It is elastic and generally of a thread-like structure, which is insoluble in water, but softens when exposed to the air, and becomes viscid, brown, and semi-transparent. See § 46.

fil'ament. A separate fiber of a nerve, or other tissue.

fermenta'tion. The transformation of any organic substance into new compounds by the action of minute living organisms, or by that of certain unorganized substances. There are many kinds of fermentation:

Alcoholic fermentation, or "vinous fermentation," is produced by the presence of various microscopic plants, or *fungi*. Under favorable conditions, in solutions containing sugar, they increase very rapidly, and decompose such solutions into carbonic acid and alcohol. All of the nutritive elements of the substance are destroyed, the carbonic acid escapes into the atmosphere, and alcohol, which is not only totally useless as nutriment, but destructive to all forms of life, remains. See § 99.

Acetous fermentation is caused by the vinegar-plant, and takes place in liquids which have already undergone alcoholic fermentation. *Lactic fermentation*, or the souring of milk, is caused by minute living organisms, called *bacteria*. *Putrefactive fermentation*, or putrefaction, occurs in dead, animal tissues, and in certain plant products, and is produced by various forms of bacteria.

foll'icles. Small glandular tubes. See § 135.

food. That which when eaten supplies nourishment to the body. See §§ 91–101.

func'tion. The particular action, or mode of operation, which is proper to any organ.

gan'glion. A knot or enlargement on a nerve or lymphatic.

gas'tric. Pertaining to the stomach. *Gastric juice,* an important digestive fluid secreted by the peptic glands. See § 110.

germs. Microscopic organisms, especially of injurious kinds. See § 213.

gland. A smooth, rounded part, or organ, which secretes or excretes some substance peculiar to itself. The liver is the largest gland in the body. Other glands are, the pancreas, the salivary glands, the lacrymal glands, etc.

glot'tis. The opening between the pharynx and the larynx. See § 74.

glu'ten. The nitrogenous part of various grain foods. See § 95.

gray matter. The gray, or ash-colored, portion of the nervous system. See § 146.

heart. See §§ 50–64.

hem'orrhage (hem' or age). Bleeding; a discharge of blood from the blood-vessels. See § 68.

hy'giene (hī' ji ēn). A system of principles, or rules, for the preservation of health.

inorgan'ic. Not having the organization of parts which characterizes living bodies; not possessing life. See § 6.

intes'tines. The lower part of the alimentary or digestive canal. The small intestine is smooth and tubular, and is twenty to twenty-five feet in length. The large intestine is more or less sacculated, and is about five feet in length. See §§ 102, 120–128.

invol'untary mus'cles. Muscles that are not under the control of the will. See § 22.

i'ris. The colored curtain between the cornea of the eye and the crystalline lens. See §§ 169, 175.

jaun'dice (jän'dis). A disease in which the yellow bile pigments are in the blood, thus giving a yellow tinge to the skin and the whites of the eyes. See § 124.

lab'yrinth. The principal portion of the internal ear. See § 185.

lac'rymal. Of, or pertaining to, tears. See § 162.

lac'teals. Minute tubes which absorb the chyle from the small intestine, and convey it into the circulation. See § 129.

lar'ynx. The upper part of the trachea, in which vocal sounds are made and modulated. See § 74.

lens. A transparent substance bounded by two curved surfaces (usually spherical), or by a curved surface and a plane surface. Rays of light passing through it are bent from their original direction. Artificial lenses are commonly made of glass. The most perfect example of a natural lens is the crystalline lens of the eye. All convex lenses are thicker at the center and thinner at the circumference. A double convex lens is one in which both of the surfaces are spherical and curve outward from the center, thus, (). In a double convex lens, like the crystalline lens of the eye, the rays of light are converged to a point beyond, called the *focus*. See § 174.

lig'ament. A band of tissue, binding one part to another.

liv'er. The largest gland in the body. See § 120.

lungs. The chief organs of respiration. See §§ 76–90.

lymph. An alkaline fluid of a yellowish color. It is very similar, in appearance and composition, to the blood deprived of its red corpuscles and diluted with water. See § 127.

lymphat'ics (lim fat'ics). Small transparent vessels, existing in various tissues of the body. Like the veins, they are provided with valves, which permit the matter which they carry to flow only toward the heart. They convey lymph, and those which run from the intestines also take up some of the chyle, and are there called *lacteals*. See § 130.

lymphat'ic glands. Small bodies through which the lymphatics pass on their way toward the thoracic duct. They vary in size, from that of a pin-head to that of an almond. See definition of *gland* above. See § 130.

mar'row. The soft tissue found in the interior of many of the bones. In the long bones of the arms and legs it is of a yellowish color, and consists of about ninety-five per cent. of fat. In various other bones it is of a reddish hue, is much softer, and contains but a small proportion of fat. See § 7. The spinal cord is not marrow, but a tissue of an entirely different character. See § 160.

masse'ter mus'cle. The principal muscle which moves the lower jaw. See §§ 27, 106.

mastication. The act of chewing. See § 103.

medul'la oblonga'ta. That portion of the brain which is continuous with the spinal cord. See § 159.

mid'dle ear. See § 184.

mem'brane. An expansion of any soft tissue, or part, in the form of a thin layer, generally covering or lining some other part.

mu'cous mem'brane. The soft, velvety lining of the alimentary canal, and of all the cavities of the body which communicate with the air. At the openings of the body it blends with, and is continuous with, the skin. See § 72.

mu'cus. The viscid fluid secreted by the mucous membrane. See § 72.

mus'cles. The flesh, or "lean meat" of the animal body. See §§ 20–29.

narcot'ic. A substance which blunts the senses, deadens sensibility, induces sleep, and, in large quantities, produces complete insensibility, The most typical of narcotics is opium. See § 166. See also, definition of *stimulant*, below.

nasal (nā'zal). Pertaining to the nose.

nerve. The name usually applied to a nerve-fiber, or bundle of nerve-fibers. See § 147.

nerve-cell. Any cell composing a part of the nervous system. See § 146.

nerve-cen'ter. A group of nerve-cells closely connected with one another, and acting together for the performance of some particular function. See § 146.

nerve-fi'ber. A very minute cord, the function of which is to convey impressions to, or from, some central portion of the nervous system. See § 146.

nerve-tis'sue, or nervous tissue. The tissue of which the nervous system is composed. It includes the nerve-fibers and the nerve-cells. See § 146.

ni'trogen. A colorless, odorless, tasteless gas, which forms about seventy-seven per cent. of the air, by weight. See § 83.

nitro'genized foods. Nutritive substances containing nitrogen. See § 96.

non-nitro'genized foods. Nutritive substances which contain no nitrogen. See § 97.

nutri'tion. The process of absorbing into the system such food as will build up and repair the living tissues. See § 90.

olfact'ory nerve. The nerve of smell. See § 189.

o'pium. The juice of the opium-poppy thickened by evaporation. In small quantities it is a stimulant-narcotic, and is largely used in medicines. In larger quantities, or when taken frequently into the system, it is a narcotic poison. See § 165.

op'tic. Pertaining to the eye, or to the sense of sight. *Optic nerve.* See § 170.

or'bit. The bony cavity which contains the eye.

or'gan. A part, or member of the body, by means of which some vital process is carried on: as the organs of digestion, of circulation, etc.

organism. An individual belonging to the animal or vegetable kingdom, and therefore possessing organs.

ox'ygen. A colorless, odorless, tasteless gas which forms about twenty-three per cent. of the air, by weight. See § 83.

pan'creas. A large gland near the stomach, the function of which is to secrete pancreatic juice. See § 125.

pancreat'ic juice. A clear, viscid fluid which aids in intestinal digestion, particularly in the digestion of the fats and starch. See § 125.

papil'la. A minute, threadlike projection, generally soft in texture, and sensitive. See § 190.

par'asite. An animal that lives in, or on, or at the expense of another animal. See § 119.

parot'id. The largest of the salivary glands. See § 107.

pep'sin. The organic principle of the gastric juice, and a very important ingredient of the digestive fluids. See § 113.

perios'teum. The dense, fibrous membrane which surrounds the bones in the living body. See § 7.

perspira'tion. The liquid excreted from the skin. See § 136.

phar'ynx. A muscular membraneous cavity at the back of the mouth. It is continuous below with the esophagus, and above with the mouth, nasal passages, and eustachian tube, while it also opens near its front into the larynx. See § 73.

physiol'ogy. The science which relates to the functions or uses of the different parts and organs of the body. *Human physiology* relates specially to man. *Animal physiology* is a more general term, and is applied to the study of the physical functions, not only in man, but in all animals. *Vegetable physiology* relates to the functions of the various parts of plants.

pig'mentary matter. Organic coloring matter. See § 133.

plas'ma. The liquid part of the blood before coagulation. See § 43. See also definition of *serum*, below.

pleu'ra. The serous membrane that invests the lungs, and lines the walls of the chest. See § 76.

pul'monary. Pertaining to the lungs.

pulse. The series of beats, or pulsations, in any blood-vessel caused by the contractions of the heart. See § 57.

pu'pil. The hole, or opening, in the center of the iris, for the passage of light into the eye. See § 168.

respira'tion. The act of breathing. See §§ 71, 79.

ret'ina. The innermost coat of the eye, consisting of an expansion and modification of the optic nerve. See § 168.

sali'va. Spittle; the fluid secreted by the salivary glands. See §§ 107, 108.

sal'ivary glands. See § 105.

sclerot'ic coat. The dense white membrane continuous with the cornea, the two forming the external coat of the eye. See § 168.

seba'ceous glands. Glands of small size, secreting an oily substance which lubricates the hair and skin. See § 137.

secre'tion. The process of preparing and separating substances usually necessary for the activity and health of the body. Also a substance so prepared and separated. The glands are the principal organs of secretion.

se'rous mem'brane. A thin, delicate, but strong, membrane which lines those cavities of the body that do not communicate with the air. It secretes *serous fluid*.

se′rum. The pale-yellow liquid which exudes from the clot in coagulation of blood. It is not the same as plasma. See definition of *plasma*, above.

spi′nal col′umn. The backbone. See § 14.

spi′nal cord. The nerve substance which extends through the canal of the spinal cord. See §§ 160–162.

spi′nal nerves. The thirty-one pairs of nerves which have their origin in the spinal cord, together with all their branches. See § 161.

sprain. A violent straining or wrenching of the parts surrounding a joint, not resulting in a dislocation. See § 19.

spu′tum. Saliva; spittal; the product of expectoration. See § 213.

stim′ulant. A substance which, taken into the system, temporarily produces increased vital action in one or more of the tissues. Some stimulants act directly on the tissues, some excite the nerves which control their action, others paralyze or restrain the nerves. Alcohol and tobacco are stimulants, exciting the nerves and tissues to unnatural, and therefore, unhealthy and destructive action. See definition of *narcotic*, above. See *alcohol*.

stom′ach. See §§ 112–119.

struct′ure. A term used in physiology to denote some organic form, or some special organization of parts or tissues.

styp′tic. A substance which, by its astringent qualities, acts toward the checking of hemorrhage. See § 68.

subling′ual. Salivary glands under the tongue. See § 107.

submax′illary. Salivary glands under the jaws. See § 107.

su′ture. An immovable joint, or line of union, like those between the bones of the skull. See § 17.

sympathet′ic sys′tem. That portion of the nervous system which controls the involuntary functions of the various organs. See § 151.

sys′tem. When used in its widest, or most general sense, this word indicates the entire body, regarded as a physiological unity. In such case we say *the* system.

Used in a more restricted sense, it refers to an assemblage of parts or organs concurring in the performance of some particular function. The principal systems of the body, in this sense are the *digestive system*, the *circulatory system*, the *respiratory system*, etc.

Used in a still more restricted sense, this word refers to an assemblage of parts or organs having a similar structure, or composed of the same, or similar, tissues. The principal systems in this sense are the *osseous*, including the bones and cartilages; the *muscular*, both voluntary and involuntary; the *vascular*, including the blood-vessels and the lymphatics; the *tegumentary*, including the skin and its appendages; the *mucous*, embracing the mucous membranes; the *serous*, embracing the serous membranes; and the *nervous*, including the sympathetic and the cerebro-spinal systems.

ten'don. A band of dense fibrous tissue, generally continuous at one end with the periosteum, or fibrous covering of a bone, and at the other with the tissues which invest or compose a muscle. See § 23.

thorac'ic duct (tho ras'ik). The tube or canal which conveys the greater part of the lymph and a portion of the chyle into the circulation. Its average length in adults is from fifteen to eighteen inches, and its diameter is about equal to that of a goose-quill. It lies along the front of the spinal column, extending to the root of the neck, where it ends in a large vein. It has three coats, and, like the veins, is provided with valves. See § 130.

tho'rax. The chest. See § 14.

tis'sue. The fabric, or particular substance, composing any organ. For description of the principal tissues in the human body, see §§ 20, 21.

tra'chea (trā' ke a). The windpipe. See § 75.

trichina (tri ki'na). A minute parasitic worm, sometimes found in the flesh of swine, and certain other animals. See § 119.

tym'panum. The middle ear, including both its cavity, its contents, and its walls. See §§ 183, 184.

va'so-mo'tor nerves. The nerves which are supplied to the muscular coat of the blood-vessels. See § 150.

vein. One of a set of canals, or tubes, the function of which is to convey the blood to the heart. See § 61.

ve'na ca'va. Either of the two large veins which discharge the blood into the right ventricle of the heart. See § 61.

ventila'tion. The theory and art of supplying buildings, etc., with pure air. See § 87.

ven'tricle. Some small cavity of the body. The *ventricles of the heart* are the two cavities which receive the blood from the auricles, and force it into the arteries. See § 51. There are also other ventricles, as *ventricles of the brain, olfactory ventricles*, etc., the description of which is not essential to an elementary knowledge of physiology.

ver'tebra. One of the bones of which the spinal column is composed. See § 14.

vil'li. Minute projections on the inner surface of the small intestine. See § 129.

vit'reous hu'mor. The transparent, jelly-like fluid which fills about four-fifths of the eyeball, or the entire space behind the crystalline lens. See § 169.

vo'cal cords. The borders of two folds of mucous membrane within the larynx, the vibration of which produces vocal sound. See § 74.

vol'untary mus'cles. The muscles that are controlled by the will. See § 22.

white matter. That portion of the nervous tissue which serves to transmit nerve force, but does not originate it. See § 146.

www.ingramcontent.com/pod-product-compliance
Lightning Source LLC
Chambersburg PA
CBHW030550040726
47497CB00008B/2654